THE BARFTASTIC LIFE OF LOUIE BURGER

CLASS B.U.R.P.

by **JENNY MEYERHOFF**

with pictures by **JASON WEEK**

o o o o o o o o o o o o o o o o o o Farrar Straus Giroux o New York

For
Jenna, Danny, Jonny, and Sam.
Elena, Jake, Zach, Lily, Ethan, and Jonah.

Farrar Straus Giroux Books for Young Readers
175 Fifth Avenue, New York 10010

Text copyright © 2014 by Jenny Meyerhoff
Art copyright © 2014 by Jason Week
All rights reserved
Printed in the United States of America
by RR Donnelley & Sons Company, Harrisonburg, Virginia
Designed by Andrew Arnold
First edition, 2014
1 3 5 7 9 10 8 6 4 2

mackids.com

Library of Congress Cataloging-in-Publication Data
Meyerhoff, Jenny.
    The barftastic life of Louie Burger : class B.U.R.P. / Jenny Meyerhoff ;
pictures by Jason Week. — First edition.
        pages cm.
    Summary: After a video of fifth grader Louie Burger is aired on a
comedy television show, Louie hopes that he will no longer be a Boy Used
to Ridicule and Put-downs (B.U.R.P.), but his popularity is very short-lived.
    ISBN 978-0-374-30521-5 (hardback)
    ISBN 978-0-374-30523-9 (ebook)
    [1. Popularity—Fiction.   2. Comedians—Fiction.   3. Family life—
Fiction.   4. Friendship—Fiction.   5. Schools—Fiction.   6. Humorous
stories.]   I. Week, Jason, ill.   II. Title.

PZ7.M571753Bav 2014
[Fic]—dc23
                                                        2013041363

Farrar Straus Giroux Books for Young Readers may be purchased for
business or promotional use. For information on bulk purchases please
contact Macmillan Corporate and Premium Sales Department at
(800) 221-7945 x5442 or by email at specialmarkets@macmillan.com.

THE PERKS OF BEING A BARFBURGER

I hike my backpack high on my shoulders and take one last bite of the caramel apple my dad let me eat for breakfast. It's a Monday morning in the middle of October and the leaves are starting to change colors, but it's not cold yet. I step outside without a coat. My sweatshirt is enough. Besides, it's a Lou Lafferman sweatshirt. I don't want my coat to cover it. In case no one at school watched *Lou Lafferman's Laff Night* on Friday night and noticed a certain viewer video with a certain orange-haired kid. Or in case no one watched the local news and saw a story about a certain kid who got to be on TV. If they don't see my sweatshirt, people might not realize there is someone sort of famous in their class. Me.

"What do you want to be for Halloween?" I ask Nick as I meet him on my driveway and we start our walk to Barker Elementary School.

"I don't know." Nick jumps in a pile of leaves left at the edge of our neighbors' lawn, then he pushes the leaves back together and catches up with me. "We're going to trick-or-treat with Thermos, right?"

"Barf course," I say. Making up new words by adding *barf* is part of my comedy shtick. Shtick is like a comedy routine. After I got the stomach flu a couple weeks ago, I thought about changing my shtick, but I decided barf is a classic. You don't mess with a classic. "I wonder what Thermos will be."

Nick has been my best friend since forever, and Thermos is a newie but a goodie. We are a great trio. Suddenly it hits me. "We should do a three-way costume!" I've never done matching costumes before.

"I'm going to be a unicorn," my little sister, Ruby, chimes in. Nick and I have to walk our younger siblings to school, but mostly we ignore them. "My unicorn name will be Cornelia Rubicornica."

I stop walking and drop my jaw in fake surprise. Ruby is wearing a homemade unicorn T-shirt and a pair of gym shoes my dad let her decorate with googly eyes and cardboard unicorn horns. Her brain is probably shaped like a unicorn because she spends so much time thinking about them.

"I never would have guessed you'd be a unicorn."

I smack my palm against my forehead. "Are you sure you're not going to be a banana?"

"I'm going to be a banana!" Henry, Nick's younger brother, jumps up and down as he walks beside us. "We already ordered my costume from the Internet store!"

"You should be a banana unicorn," Ruby says. "I'll make you a horn and your name can be Banoonicorn."

Henry's eyes go wide. "Thank you."

"Original," I say, and Nick and I smile at each other. Little kids can be built-in entertainment when they aren't barfnoying you to death.

We reach the corner and the crossing guard holds up his stop sign for us to cross the street to our school.

"We could be the three dimensions for Halloween," I suggest to Nick. "Length, width, and height. Or we could all be C-3PO, from Star Wars. We'll wear the letters *PO* on our chests and when people ask us what we are we'll answer: 'What do you see? Three POs. We're See-3-POs.'"

Nick and I walk over to the fifth-grade blacktop as Ruby and Henry join the first graders. Each grade gathers in a different section of the playground before the morning bell rings.

"Those are good ideas." Nick wrinkles one side of his nose. "I'm just not sure everyone will get them. Maybe we should keep brainstorming."

"Sure," I tell him. "I'll keep a list."

As we get closer to the fifth graders, I notice at least twenty-five kids huddled around the tetherball pole. Almost as many kids as the time I pretended to be a ninja delivering a roundhouse kick to my mortal enemy Melonhead and my ankle got completely tangled in the tetherball string. I had to stand on one foot for about fifteen minutes until JoAnne, the school custodian, arrived to cut me down and walk me to the nurse's office with the tetherball bouncing along behind my ankle like an old-timey prisoner's ball and chain.

Um, I take it back. That didn't actually happen. *Really.*

It's weird to see so many people, from *all* three

of the fifth-grade classes, standing around the pole, because they haven't even replaced the tetherball yet. What are they watching? Is it a pole-staring contest? When the kids see Nick and me, I worry they are angry about the missing ball, but a bunch of them smile and wave Nick over.

Even though Nick and I are best friends, he's got a lot of other friends besides me. The only friend I have besides him is Thermos.

"Come on!" a kid named Grant shouts. A girl named Ava wiggles her fingers in our direction.

"Uh, I think Ava waved at you," I say.

"Really?" Nick smiles funny, but then he looks at the ground and doesn't wave back.

"Come on," Grant calls again.

"Go ahead," I tell Nick. "I've got a joke book in my backpack to keep me company."

Nick raises an eyebrow. "You should come, too. We could all hang out together."

It sounds like a reasonable suggestion, but if I go hang out with Nick and the other kids, I might misunderstand when one of them starts talking about the Bears. Then I might do my grizzlies-eating-cafeteria-food impression, but no one will get it because they will be thinking about football players, not wild animals, and Nick will have to explain what I'm doing and everyone will say, "Oh, funny," but they won't mean it.

"Louie!" Grant calls my name. "Come here! We've been waiting for you."

I glance over my shoulder to see if Grant is talking to some other Louie standing right behind me. I can't remember anyone beckoning me before. I check to see if Ryan Rakefield is standing with them, because if he is, then I'll know it's a trick, but he's nowhere in sight. He must not be at school yet.

"Come on," another kid shouts, and Nick grabs my arm and drags me with him because I'm kind of in shock.

"Cool shirt," Grant says when we get to the tetherball pole. "Did Lou Lafferman give that to you?"

I shake my head. "I had it from before. Lou is my favorite comedian. I tape his show every night."

"Lucky!" says a girl from Mrs. Wolf's class. "I'm not allowed to watch it until I'm twelve."

"Me neither," says Grant. "But I saw the video of you on the Internet. My parents let me watch it after they heard about you on the news."

My head is spinning trying to keep up with the different kids talking to me. They are circled around me, and Nick is right next to me, but I'm the one everyone is talking to. A girl from my third-grade reading group tells me that she's played my video twenty-seven times. She asks me to autograph her backpack. I wrap my arm across my stomach and pinch my waist. It hurts, so I know I must be awake.

Whenever I read about people pinching themselves to see if they are dreaming, I always think that sounds fake. I mean, come on, who doesn't know if they are dreaming? But today, for the very first time, I understand. Nothing like this has ever happened in my life before. Everyone is talking to me, and looking at me, surrounding me, but it's not to make fun of me or laugh at something I did. It's because they think I'm cool. They think I'm S.W.A.G.: Someone Worth Acknowledging and Greeting. It's unbarflievable.

I feel light-headed, not like I'm going to faint, but like I'm going to float away in a cloud. Visions of being carried through the hallways on the shoulders of my classmates fill my head.

"So what do you think?" Grant asks me.

"About what?" I was so busy being happy, I forgot to pay attention to what everyone was saying.

"About lunch." Grant nods enthusiastically.

I look at Nick and raise my eyebrows, hoping he'll know what's so great about lunch, but he shrugs at me, so I say, "I think lunch is one of the three best meals of the day."

Grant laughs, but I barely hear him, because from across the playground a different voice coats my skin with ice. "Don't stand too close! Barf burger might hurl on you!"

I look up and see Ryan Rakefield walking over with Thermos and a bunch of other fifth graders from bus 54. Ryan shouts, "I can smell him from here."

I cringe and look at Grant, ready for him to hold his nose, take a giant step backward, and call me Barf burger. A couple of kids look at me suspiciously, but Grant says, "So, do you actually know Lou now? Could you call him on the phone?"

I shake my head. I can't speak and my heart is pounding. I'm sure the teasing is going to start any second. Ryan and Thermos elbow their way to the center of the crowd. Ryan sneers at me. "I could have been on that show if I wanted, but no one watches *Lou Lafferman* anymore. My parents say that *The Bobby Duffy Show* is way funnier."

"I watch Lou." Thermos dribbles her basketball hard as she talks, then swings her right leg over the ball as it bounces. She's got moves coming out of her ears, but the boys still won't let her play with them at recess.

"Me, too," says Nick. "I love Lou. He's going to be in a movie soon, *Snow White and the Seven Dorks*. He's playing Snow White."

"I hope my parents let me see it," Grant says as the first bell rings.

Most of the kids by the tetherball pole wander away to pick up their backpacks from where they dropped them when they got to school. I never put mine down, so I head straight to Mrs. Adler's line-up spot. Ryan passes by me and bumps me hard on my shoulder. My backpack slides down my arm and I trip and fall into Jamal.

"Watch it, barf bag!" Ryan says, even though *he* bumped *me*. He runs the rest of the way to the line without looking back.

"Are you okay?" Thermos asks.

"I'm fine." I stand up, and Jamal hands me my

backpack. I reach my hand out slowly, waiting for the trick. Is he going to pull it away? Throw it over my head? But when I'm holding on to the strap Jamal simply lets go and walks away.

Weird.

"Actually," I tell Thermos, "I'm better than fine."

More than twenty kids just talked to me like I was a regular student. I hold my head high and walk into school, down the fifth-grade hall, and over to my locker. Except for the day when the video of me barfing on stage at the fifth-grade talent show aired on national television, today is the most barftastic day of my life.

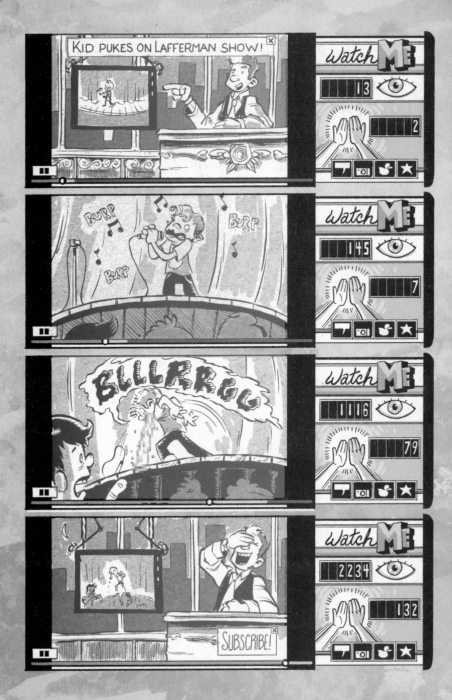

STICKY PALMS AND COWBOY BOOTS

On Tuesday afternoon, for the first time ever, I walk into gym class without a feeling of *total* dread and despair. It's more like medium dread with a sprinkling of despair. Gym is normally the place where my lowly status is the most noticeable. Usually, unless Nick or Thermos is a team captain, I can pretty much guarantee that I'm going to get picked last. Today, I'm not sure what to expect. So many things have been different lately.

Yesterday morning, Grant asked me to be partners for spelling tests. Yesterday afternoon, Owen asked Nick, Thermos, and me if he could join our game of Time-Travel Pinecones at recess. And today, when Hannah got to choose someone to walk with her to the office for photocopies, she chose me. That was sort of embarrassing, because her friends kept giggling. But it was way better than being embarrassed for getting a wad of red tissue paper stuck in your nose because you were trying to make yourself look like a fire-breathing warlock.

Not that that actually happened. *Really.*

So even though it seems like things are looking up, I can't trust that it's real until I've made it through a gym class without becoming a laughing-stock.

Class starts with two laps around the gym, like always. I try to keep my head held high, but I trip, and Mr. Lamb tells me to stop staring at the ceiling while I jog. I think I hear a snigger, but it could have been someone's gym shoe squeaking. After laps, I join my class on the blue line. We're going to be picking teams soon. I barely have any butterflies in my stomach. Maybe one or two caterpillars, but that's it. I'm sure gym won't be the horror it used to be. My days of being class B.U.R.P. (Boy Used to Ridicule and Put-downs) are nearly over.

Mr. Lamb blows his whistle and I practically feel a gust of wind on my face. He must have an electric whistle or something. Everyone gets quiet, and Mr. Lamb clasps his hands behind his back. "We are about to begin my favorite unit of the year!" he barks. "One that will serve you well in all your future endeavors. I will match each of you with a new partner for this unit only. There will be no complaining."

Well, we're not picking teams, so that's good, but that's the only positive I can find. If our new unit is Mr. Lamb's favorite, it's going to be torturous. We're probably going to do Greco-Roman wrestling or kickboxing or ultimate fighting. There's a theme there, get it? One thousand and one ways for Louie Burger to get squished. I hope I don't get Ryan Rakefield as my partner. I cross my eyes and my fingers. My legs are already crossed. *Not Ryan Rakefield.*

Mr. Lamb walks into the supply closet and when he walks back out, he's no longer wearing shoes. He's still wearing his gym shorts, his hoodie, and his whistle, but we can see every inch of his sweat socks, even the yellow stitching on the toes. I put my hand over my mouth so Mr. Lamb doesn't see me smile. Without his gym shoes, he looks practically naked. And old, like a grandpa wearing underpants.

In his hands, Mr. Lamb carries two cowboy boots. He raises one boot up high. "As you might be able to guess, it's time for square-dancing. This boot has the names of the boys and this one has the names of the girls." He holds up the other one, then he puts both boots on the floor and pulls a name from each. "Theodora Albertson and Ryan Rakefield!"

Next to me I hear Thermos huff out a breath. I give her a look of sympathy. It would have been bad enough kickboxing Ryan, but dancing with him? I can't think of anything worse.

"It's your lucky day!" Ryan stands up and takes a bow. Thermos does not look impressed. Mr. Lamb ignores him. Or maybe he doesn't hear because he's shouting the next pairs.

"Jamal Thomas and Lauren Faber. Nick Yama-shita and Grace Fairweather. Louie Burger and Ava Gonzales."

After Mr. Lamb calls Ava's name and mine, a bunch of girls start giggling. I look over at Nick and make my funniest yuck face, but Nick doesn't laugh. He looks back and forth between Grace and Ava. Mr. Lamb finishes calling out the rest of the names, then tells us to stand with our partners. There are a bunch of squares taped on the floor. The boys are to stand in the red squares and the girls in the green.

I walk over to Ava on the other side of the gym, and she steps into her green square and waits for me. I try to smile, but only one half of my mouth works. I feel lopsided and strange, like the time I accidentally brought my dad's bathing suit to the water park and had to spend the whole day hold-ing it up with both hands. I thought slam-crash-smush ball was the worst thing that could happen in gym. I was wrong. Square-dancing is definitely worse. I drag my feet into the red square, ready for disaster.

"Before we begin, you need to learn some basic moves. Jamal and Lauren, come up front to dem-onstrate."

Jamal and Lauren walk to the front of the class. They stand about a million feet apart from each other.

"Rule number one!" Mr. Lamb shouts. "You have to touch your partner. No covering your hand with your shirt or air touching. And no saying *ew* or *yuck* or anything else negative! You will be ladies and gentlemen! Now, demonstrators, bow to your partner."

Jamal and Lauren both bow.

"The first move you need to know is called promenade. Stand shoulder to shoulder and hold both hands, left with left and right with right."

Jamal and Lauren hold hands. A bunch of girls titter, and I almost groan, but Mr. Lamb stares his most drill sergeant-y stare at us.

"Now walk forward to the music like this." Mr. Lamb puts on his boots and moseys forward like a cowboy. Jamal does the same. Mr. Lamb looks impressed. "Have you square-danced before?" he asks.

Jamal shakes his head.

"Well, that was mighty good, pardner." Mr. Lamb does a fake cowboy voice that sounds strange coming from a person in a gray hoodie. "You're a natural-born dancer."

Ryan sniggers, and so do a bunch of other kids in the room. Jamal scuffs his shoe on the floor. Thermos rolls her eyes at me from behind Ryan's back.

"Now, everyone," Mr. Lamb continues in his regular bark, "bow to your partner and grab hands. We're going to promenade around the room. Watch Jamal if you want to know how it's supposed to look!"

Ava and I bow to each other and I smack my forehead against her cheek. She giggles, but I don't see what's funny. My head actually hurts. We grab hands and I realize there is something sticky on my palm. Maybe leftover jelly from lunch? I want to wipe it on my pants, but Ava's holding too tightly and Mr. Lamb has already turned on the music and I don't want anyone else to notice.

Ava and I promenade around the gym. I trip a couple of times, but only knock us both to the floor once. I scramble up quickly, but everyone is so pre-occupied with the weirdness of holding hands that nobody notices except Nick. He's got his eyes glued on Ava and me, probably so he won't have to look at Grace.

Ryan keeps letting go of Thermos's hands and she keeps grabbing back on. We make it through the rest of the promenade without anyone laughing or pointing. I breathe a sigh of relief. Next we learn do-si-dos and elbow swings and finally, thank goodness, we bow to each other one more

time (this time I bump my forehead on Ava's shoulder) and line up.

I race to get in line by Nick and Thermos. "This was the worst gym class in the history of gym classes," Nick whispers. "Square-dancing is so dumb."

"What are you complaining about?" Thermos moans. "I had to dance with Ryan. His palms were sticky!" Thermos says that last part really loud.

"Yeah, it would be better with a good partner. *You* got a good partner," Nick says to me. Then his cheeks turn pink and he looks at the floor. "I mean, Ava's not horrible."

"There is no such thing as a good partner," I remind Nick. I rub my hands against my pants, and shoot a glance back at Ava. I wonder if she will tell everyone I have sticky palms. If she does, the teasing will start, and this won't be my best gym class ever anymore.

Everyone in my class waits in line patiently for Mrs. Adler, except for Ryan. He saunters up and down beside us in a fake cowboy walk, then pretends to tip his hat to Ava. "Why, hello there, ma'am." He walks over to Thermos. "Howdy, sir."

Mr. Lamb steers Ryan back in line and says, "You need more bounce in your step. Ask Jamal over there to give you some pointers. Or your partner, she's not too bad herself."

Thermos puffs up her chest, but Ryan's cheeks turn pink. He fake smiles at her, then at Jamal, and his eyes narrow. "What do you say, *pardner*? Are you going to wear your cowboy boots tomorrow, like Mr. Lamb?"

Jamal glances at Thermos, then turns and stares straight ahead as Mrs. Adler arrives to take us back to class. The whole way, I can hear Ryan whispering to Jamal: "Look at that bounce in your step. You're a natural-born dancer."

Thermos taps me on the shoulder. "I sure wish someone would teach him a lesson."

I nod, but inside I'm too busy cheering. I can't believe it. I actually went an entire gym class without getting teased!

THE FUTURE by LOUIE BURGER

WORSE THAN GYM

After school, Nick and Thermos come over to my house. The front yard is full of leaves, but it's warm, so we decide to hang out outside. We play Worse Than Gym, where we have to invent an activity worse than what we did in gym. This time we each make up a kind of dance that is worse than square-dancing. Thermos's dance is called basketbancing. It's a cross between basketball and dancing, without a ball. First we act like we're dribbling, then we spin. Then we pretend like we're shooting, then we lunge back in a dip. It looks ridiculous and cracks us up, like it's supposed to. Nick's dance is called the B.L.T. Instead of Bacon, Lettuce, and Tomato, the letters stand for the

Booty Leg Tap. Basically you try to tap your booty with your legs in a rhythmic way. It's much harder than it sounds.

Finally, I teach them rhombus dancing. It's a lot like square-dancing, only you have to squish yourself down while you dance, because a rhombus looks like a squished square. We do a promenade like ducks waddling across the grass, but I stand up when I realize Jamal is out on his front lawn down the street watching us. Did you ever notice that most really fun activities look bizarre to the people who don't know what you are doing?

Jamal has lived on the same street as Nick and me for three years, but we never hang out with him. When Jamal first moved in, his mom invited me over for lunch one day and she served macaroni and cheese with cut-up pieces of hot dog. Jamal and I played Chipmunk Paratroopers and it was kind of fun, but the next week he started hanging out with Ryan, and now we both pretend that day never happened. He watches me from his lawn a lot though. Probably so that he can report back to Ryan and laugh at me.

"What's wrong?" Nick looks up at me from his waddling-duck position. "Did you think of a new dance?"

I shake my head as I watch Jamal climb on his bicycle and head up our street. Thermos and Nick stand, too, and we watch Jamal ride up the block and back down. He looks over at us, but no one says anything.

After that, Thermos, Nick, and I go inside my house and watch old Three Stooges videos on the Internet until it's time for them to go home.

After dinner, my dad claps his hands. "There's a chill in the air and the leaves are falling. You know what time it is!"

"Spooky Farms!" Ruby jumps out of her chair and high-fives my dad.

"Do I have to go?" Ari, my older sister, asks. She and I used to hang out all the time, but then she started middle school. Now she doesn't want to do anything unless she's with at least seventeen friends.

"Of course you do," my mother says. "We can't have our family tradition without the entire family."

Every fall, my family visits the Spooky Farms Pumpkin Patch Halloween Headquarters to start getting ready for Halloween. Halloween is a pretty big deal to my dad. He calls October Halloween Month. For thirty-one days he eats candy corn for dessert, answers the phone with "helloween," and wears jack-o'-lantern underpants.

My dad hurries us into our jackets and herds us to the car. For the entire ride he makes us sing along to "Monster Mash," and when we arrive at Spooky Farms he marches us straight to the haunted corn maze, his favorite part, and buys five tickets.

We have to split up because the guy at the front of the maze won't let in groups larger than four. Mom and Ari go in first.

"Okay, who will hold my hand?" Dad acts like he's totally scared, even though Ruby's the one who usually freaks out. Last year she screamed the entire time.

"I will, I will." Ruby grabs my dad's left hand and he holds the right one out to me, but I shake my head.

"I'm going to do it by myself this year," I tell him.

"You sure?" he asks.

I nod, and the ticket guy waves my dad and Ruby into the maze. A few minutes later he waves me in, too. At every intersection, I pick the turn that will move me away from the exit, because I don't want to finish too fast, but after a while I've lost my sense of direction.

I zip my coat up higher because the sun has set and the air is getting chilly. I have no idea how long I've been in the maze, but it's starting to feel like a very long time. At the next intersection I don't know if I should try the path to the right or the path to the left. I'm ready to be done. The outside edges of my ears are starting to freeze.

I decide to go left. I might have been at this part of the maze before, and I might have gone left here before, but it's hard to tell since all the cornstalks look the same. I head down the path and after a few paces I turn right at a corner and—

"Mwahahaha!"

A vampire lunges at me and grabs at my coat. I scream and run, tripping over my feet and landing on my knees in a patch of mud as I escape. I know the vampire won't chase me. That's the fourth time I've accidentally walked into his corner, but he startles me every time. I stand and retrace my steps until I am back at the intersection I started from, and this time I go to the right. I turn left at the shrieking bat and right at the moaning mummy. I walk through a huge cloud of fog and turn left at the tombstone and—

"Gotcha!"

A green Frankenstein clamps his beefy fingers

on my shoulders and I scream again. He lets go of me and I race back through the fog, turning left, then right, then left, and then I don't know where I am. My heart pounds so hard I think my ribs might crack. I run until I trip over a bale of hay and realize I am in a small room with cornstalk walls. Glow-in-the-dark eyes peek out from between the cornhusks. The bale of hay sits in the middle of the room like a bench. I plop down on it to figure out my next move.

The *mwahahaha*s of the vampire, the *gotcha*s of Frankenstein, and the screams and laughter of other maze-goers float over the cornstalks to my ears. Then I hear a familiar voice.

"It's been twenty minutes, David! I'm worried."

"I'm sure he's goofing around."

My parents. I can hear them. I must be close to the end of the maze. I stand up and walk over to one of the creepy eye walls.

"Mom?" I say.

No answer.

"Mom!" I scream a little louder. Someone behind me cackles. It doesn't sound like a witch's cackle. I turn slowly, the hair on the back of my neck standing at attention before I've even seen the source of the laughter.

"Are you scared, Barfburger?"

Ryan Rakefield is standing in the doorway of the eyeball room with Jamal and a couple of other guys from our class, Dustin and James. His taunts shouldn't bother me. I'm pretty sure I'm not the class B.U.R.P. anymore, but when I hear Ryan's voice, I feel like I am.

"Louie?" My mother's shouts echo over the maze. "Don't move. I'll find you!"

Ryan bugs his eyes and lets out a snort of disbelief. "Are you lost? In a kiddie maze?"

I stumble sideways, and a dried cornhusk scrapes my neck. I wish I could leave, but Ryan and his friends are blocking the way out. I unzip my jacket because suddenly the collar is pinching.

"I'm not lost." My voice squeaks.

"Didn't you call your mommy?" Ryan smirks and

so do Dustin, James, and Jamal. "And didn't your mom tell you not to move?"

I shake my head. "Uh, no." My jeans feel itchy and I wish these barf bags would go away and leave me alone. "That was my friend Mon. We're, uh, playing hide-and-seek."

"Mon?" Jamal asks.

"Yeah, it's short for Montana," I say, naming the first thing to come into my mind.

"There's no one at our school named Montana." Jamal looks at Ryan smugly.

"He's making it up," Ryan says. "Little lost baby-burger doesn't have any friends, remember?"

I open my mouth, trying to think of a great retort, a way to remind him of everyone who likes me now, a way that will make him feel like a smelly toad, but Ryan shakes his head and sneers.

"You think those kids are your real friends? They're only interested in you because you barfed on TV. In a couple more days that will be old news, and you'll go back to being a nobody."

I spin around looking for any other way out of this space, my hands shaking.

"That's not—" I start to say, but my foot lands on a mat that makes a click, and hundreds of spiders pour down on my head. I scream until I realize that they are plastic and I remember that Ryan is watching me.

"Louie!" My mother rushes to me and brushes the plastic spiders off my shoulders and hair. "Are you okay?"

"Fine," I say, trying not to make eye contact with Ryan and his posse. I straighten up and put my hand on my hip. "Uh, have you seen Montana?"

"What are you talking about?" My mother picks one last stray spider from my hair.

I push her hand away. "We better go find him. He might be lost."

"I don't think I get this joke, Louie. But your father is ready to look at the decoration shop, so no more horsing around in the maze. Let's go."

We file past the boys in the doorway, and they say hello to my mother and goodbye to me like we're old pals. But as my mom leads me out the exit of the maze, their laughter is so loud it rattles the cornstalks.

FAME AND FORTUNE

I stumble out of the maze behind my mother, and the big open field spreading out in front of me makes me feel like I just got released from prison. I blink at the brightness of the floodlights. Ruby sits on my father's shoulders next to the giant-pumpkin playhouse, and Ari is leaning against the giant pumpkin. My mother guides me toward them by the elbow. "It would be hard for anyone to do the maze alone," she whispers to me. "Ari and I would definitely have gotten lost if we hadn't had each other."

"There he is!" Ruby shouts when we are halfway across the field. "He isn't lost anymore! Louie, we thought you got eaten by the zombie."

Ari shakes her head. "Um, yeah. I was pretty sure that didn't happen."

I glance around and notice at least ten people staring at me who weren't staring before, but I'm kind of tired of being embarrassed and I'm trying to forget what Ryan said about me not having any friends, so I click my heels together and do a fake tap dance, then shake my hands in the universal ta-da motion. A couple of the starers laugh, but one of them, a man in a hunting cap, gives me a strange, questioning look.

"Let's go check out the decorations!" Dad says. "This year I want our house to be the most spook-tacular house on the block. No. The most spook-tacular house in the whole neighborhood."

We follow my dad to the decorations tent and by *we*, I mean my mom, Ari, Ruby, me, and that stranger who was looking at me funny. He's still looking at me funny.

Dad and Ruby head over to the inflatables section, while Ari takes a seat on a coffin and whips out her phone. The stranger takes a step toward me, and I duck behind my mom, who is checking out the plastic skeletons. I send a bunch of bones rattling to the floor. My mother quickly picks them up and puts them back on the shelf. "Don't break anything!" she whispers. "Do you see how expensive this stuff is?"

"Excuse me." The strange man walks over to my mother and tries to look at me over her shoulder. I wonder if he is pumpkin-farm security. Maybe he wants to take me to the pumpkin-farm detention center for questioning the way they do at the airport if you announce too loudly that you bought a Cinna*bomb* for a snack.

Um, that didn't actually happen. *Really.*

"Your son is very familiar-looking." I hide behind my mother's back again, but the man inches over and peers around her.

"Oh!" My mother turns to me and shakes her head in disbelief.

"Did I just see him on TV the other day?" the man asks.

My mother nods. "I can't believe you recognize him."

The man grabs my hand, covering the back of it with his other hand, and we shake. "You were great, kid. Truly great. I wish I'd had the courage to do something like that when I was your age."

"Uh, thanks," I tell him. "It wasn't that hard. I just caught the stomach flu from my best friend. Anyone could do it, really."

The man cracks up and slaps his thigh. "You're great!" As he walks away he laughs and slaps his thigh again.

My mother ruffles my hair. "Guess you're famous, huh?"

"I guess," I say. Ryan Rakefield didn't seem to think so.

My father bounces over, his smile bigger than a jack-o'-lantern's. "I thought of a theme for our yard this year: Haunted Forest. We can get a dozen of those plastic trees and one or two extra fog machines, so the whole yard is smoky. Then we can have creatures hiding behind every tree. I'll set up a fake swamp with a swamp creature over by the mailbox. Of course we'll need swamp lights."

My father is drooling over cool things in every corner of the store, but my mother is biting her lip. Behind my father, the man who recognized me is talking to a woman and pointing at me. I wonder if I should wave or do another tap dance or act normal. Except I've forgotten how to act normal. I put one hand on my hip and hold my chin with the other, pretending that I'm concentrating hard on my parents' conversation.

"Did you see how much those trees cost?" my mother whispers. "They're $29.99 each! We can't afford a dozen of them. I don't think we should spend more than $100 on decorations. We can't do our usual Halloween spending spree this year."

"One hundred dollars will barely decorate the front door." My father picks up a talking pumpkin, turns it over to look at the price, then puts it back on the shelf.

My mother grabs his hand. "I think you should stay focused on your art. Your recycled recycling bins could be your big break."

My dad nods thoughtfully. "Yes, but I can do both. Halloween is an important Burger tradition."

My mother opens her mouth to say something, but Ari interrupts.

"OMG, you guys!" Ari jumps up from the coffin and rushes over to us. "Emma just texted me that Louie's video now has more than ten thousand views."

"Wow." My dad blinks in surprise. "Who could be watching it that many times?"

My mother tilts her head toward the cauldron

display. "That man behind you recognized Louie and shook his hand."

My dad pushes out his bottom lip and gives me a thumbs-up. "Not too shabby, son."

At that moment, the man who shook my hand returns with a pimply teenage pumpkin-farm employee. I can tell he's an employee because of the orange shirt and pants he is wearing.

"Here he is," the man in the hunting cap says. "The kid I was telling you about."

The pumpkin-farm guy holds out his hand to me and I shake it. "It's a real honor to have you at our farm," he says, handing me a small rectangle of orange paper. "Please accept this coupon for 20 percent off your purchase. Thank you."

"Thank *you*!" my dad says as my new fan walks away. "How about that?"

My mother squeezes my shoulder. "You're having quite a night."

"So, Louie, what do you want to get?" My dad points one finger over and over again at the trees. "Anything you want." Point. Point.

"Can I get one of the deluxe costumes?" Ari looks longingly at the costume tent on the other side of the pumpkin field. "My friends and I are going as pretty witches and most of them are getting fancy costumes."

"And they don't have unicorns," Ruby says, "but they have a giant binflatable black cat and we could buy it and name it UnicornCat and it could be my friend."

"The word is *in*flatable, honey, and we can't buy everything." Mom throws her hands up in the air. "Louie, what do *you* want?"

I look around the tent. Every single inch explodes with Halloween supplies, but I can't focus enough to choose. I wonder if this special treatment is going to happen everywhere I go from now on. Free ice cream at the ice cream store. No waiting at the barbershop. The librarian will no longer make me pay overdue fines. And Ryan Rakefield will give me compliments instead of insults.

"Can we use the coupon another day?" I ask. "I can't decide."

As my family walks back to the car, I secretly lift the orange coupon to my nose and sniff. It smells like fame and fortune. I can't wait for Ryan Rakefield to realize he was wrong about me.

THE NEW-AND-IMPROVED LOUIE

"Louie is completely famous," Ruby tells Henry as I walk them to school Wednesday morning. Nick isn't with us. He had to go to the doctor's office for a checkup. "They're probably even going to name a sandwich after him someday."

"Nick loves sandwiches!" Henry punches the air in celebration.

"I know," I tell him. "I'm his best friend, remember? But I'm not that famous. I was on TV, sure, and I do get VIP treatment at the pumpkin farm, but I'm not Lou Lafferman or anything."

Ruby leans over to Henry and speaks in a hushed voice like she's telling him something top secret and very important. "They gave him his own coupon."

"Wow." Henry looks at me like I'm a rock star. "When I grow up I want to get a coupon, too."

I reach my hand into the back pocket of my jeans and the rumpled orange paper brushes against my fingertips. I know that I won't need the coupon at school today, but I put it in my pocket anyway. I want to remember that I'm the kind of boy who gets coupons. Not the B.U.R.P. Ryan Rakefield says I am.

Ruby, Henry, and I turn the corner into the school yard, and the old familiar black cloud of panic fills my chest when I see the fifth graders standing in their groups, hanging out before school. Nick isn't here this morning. Who will I stand with?

I glance around for Thermos, but I don't see her either. Even Grant is missing, though I don't know if I am allowed to stand with his group before school anyway. Above me a flock of geese fly past, honking their goodbyes for the winter. The sound is so sad and lonely, suddenly the panic cloud swells and starts to fill my throat, too. I reach back and touch the coupon. I am S.W.A.G. I remind myself.

I'm the new Louie. If I walk over to my classmates, someone will say hi to me. Someone will ask me to stand with them. I say goodbye to Ruby and Henry and head off toward the fifth-grade area of the blacktop.

As soon as Ryan Rakefield sees me, he rushes over. Jamal and a couple of his other cronies lag behind.

"Barfburger?" Ryan shouts, pretending he can't see me. "Are you lost? Don't worry, we'll find you. We'll help you get to school."

I ignore him and keep walking toward the other fifth graders. A bunch of them look away from me like they don't notice Ryan's jokes. Others just watch.

"Look out!" Ryan lunges at me and I flinch.

He laughs. "I was trying to save you from the scary monster." He says the words in baby talk so they sound like *scawee monstew*. "What do you do when you trick-or-treat? Do your parents walk with you and hold your hands?"

More and more kids are starting to stare. Ryan

is shouting his insults at the top of his lungs. I want to unleash the perfect zinger comeback that will make him feel as insignificant as a dirty penny. I even think of a pretty good insult joke. *What do your parents do on Halloween? Use your photograph as a decoration? Or is that too scary for little kids?*

The thing is, I have no idea if my classmates are on my side.

"This is boring," Ryan says to his friends when I don't answer. "Come on, let's shoot some hoops before the bell rings."

"Louie!"

I look up and see Thermos climbing out of her mom's car and running toward me. As she runs, she pulls off the hair bow her mother makes her wear and swaps it for a baseball cap. "I missed the bus," she explains. "And my mother wouldn't let me take off my bow in the car. She didn't want me to take it off at school either, but she can't follow me around all day, so ha-ha-ha."

I laugh with Thermos and try to act like I wasn't just getting teased in front of the whole grade. "Can't you just lose them?" I ask.

"Nah. I've done that. She buys more." Thermos squints at me suspiciously. "What's the matter?"

"Nothing," I say, but my eyes dart over to the basketball court.

Thermos nods her head as if she knows exactly what must have happened without me saying a word. "Want me to go over there and slam my basketball in his face?" she asks.

I wrinkle my nose. "That's okay." What I want is for me not to feel like a B.U.R.P. every time I see Ryan. What I want is for everyone in fifth grade to choose me over Ryan. I thought I had that, but now I'm not so sure.

The bell rings and we get in line.

"Hi, Louie. Hi, Thermos," Ava says when Thermos and I step up behind her. "Where's Nick?"

Her friends instantly start giggling, even though I can't see anything funny about her question.

"At a checkup," I tell her.

"Oh." Ava makes a tiny frown, and her friend Hannah elbows her and says, "Too bad."

"Nah," I tell them. "Nick's not one of those kids who mind the doctor."

The girls giggle again and Thermos pulls me ahead of them as we walk inside. "I don't think that's what she meant when she said 'too bad,'" Thermos explains. "I think Ava likes Nick. *Like likes* him."

I pretend to barf and Thermos laughs.

"I know," she says. "Gross, right?"

"Right."

So Ava is probably only talking to me because she wants to know about Nick, but I hope that this is also proof that Ryan's prediction in the Corn Maze—that everyone would forget about me—isn't coming true. I mean, Ava's still willing to talk to me. It doesn't matter what the reason is.

After I put my backpack in my locker, I scoot three lockers over to where Ava and her friends are standing. "Hey," I say, "do you guys know what state greets the most people?"

They look at one another and shrug.

"O-HI-o!" I mime like I'm playing drums. *"Ba-dum-ching."*

Ava and her friends wrinkle their noses as if they don't get it. I try again. "What state writes the most letters?"

"The state of Envelopia?" Ava guesses.

"It has to be a real state," I tell her.

"PEN-sylvania!" Thermos shouts at us from her locker. She hangs her jacket up and slams the door shut.

"I don't get it," Hannah says. "Nobody even writes letters anymore. Don't they have computers and cell phones in Pennsylvania?"

These girls are a tough crowd, but I'm not giving up. I was on *Lou Lafferman.* I've been given a coupon. I know I can make them laugh.

"What state is the thirstiest? Missis-SIP-pi. What state is the happiest? MERRY-land."

"No more! Please," Hannah says.

"Just one more," I say. "What state got a new pet?"

Thermos walks over to us. She raises her eyebrows at me, waiting. "I give up. What state got a new pet?"

"New Hamster!"

Thermos chuckles. "What's the capital of Washington?" she asks me.

"W!" I say, and we high-five.

Ava and Hannah give each other funny looks, then walk into our classroom, but Ava turns around when she's halfway through the door. "Does Nick like those jokes?"

"Uh-huh," I tell her. "They crack him up!"

She crinkles her forehead like she's considering strange information, then walks to her desk. I reach into my back pocket for one more lucky-coupon rub. I'm not going back to class B.U.R.P. No how. No way.

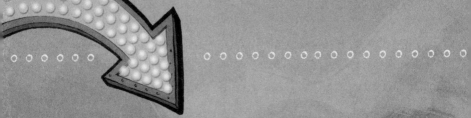

LOVEBURGERS

When I walk back out to the blacktop at lunch recess, the playground no longer feels like a dangerous jungle. First, Nick has returned from the doctor, so even though Thermos has decided to shoot hoops by herself for a while, I don't feel alone anymore. Second, I've still got my coupon. I'm about to pat my back pocket, but then I realize it will just look like I'm tapping my butt. Third, I'd completely forgotten that I am wearing all the Lou Lafferman paraphernalia that I own. Probably no one noticed it this morning because I was wearing a windbreaker, but it's warmed up, so I left my jacket inside. Now I'm sure everyone will remember that I was on TV and that I am not a B.U.R.P.

People will probably start shouting my name any second.

When Nick and I pass the edge of the blacktop, a couple of kids from Mrs. Wolf's class run over to us, and I smile because I guess my Lou Lafferman stuff did the trick. But then one of them says, "Did you guys hear? Grant Lubelcheck broke his arm!" As soon as they've made their announcement, they run off to tell more people about Grant.

Over by the tetherball pole, Grant is surrounded by a huge group of kids. His arm is in a cast, and everyone is asking him questions. I guess that's why he wasn't at school this morning.

"Come on," Nick says, dragging me over. "Let's go see what happened."

"So I climbed the tree holding my breakfast burrito in my mouth," Grant says, "and the squirrel jumped out at me, biting it from the other side. I was so startled, I let go of the trunk and fell." Grant acts out the fall. We reach the tetherball pole as he stands back up. "The squirrel ran off with the tortilla."

"You've got to video that squirrel," Grant's friend Mason says. "Wait, *was* anyone filming when you fell?"

I feel a little shaky in my stomach as I wait for Grant's answer. I know there are millions of videos on the Internet, but it kind of feels like my thing.

Grant shakes his head. "Too bad, right? I could have gone viral like Louie."

My breath flows out in a huge *ah*. I'm still the only one. And Grant remembers how barfcredible my video was. "Being viral is really cool," I say. "The other day someone—"

"Hey!" Grant cuts me off. "Who wants to sign my cast?"

Everyone shouts and elbows one another to be the first in line to sign. I get in line, too, because I don't want to be the only one not signing. When it's my turn I write *Barf-cast-ic!* and sign my name. I wait to see if anyone notices what I wrote. To see if anyone remembers my catchphrase. No one mentions it.

So I decide to ask if anyone wants to see my coupon.

"Step right up, step right up!" I pretend to be a barker at a carnival. "This is your chance to see the most amazing, the most wonderful, the most barfpendous coupon in the entire world! Meet me by the rock wall."

I hold my coupon high in the air as I march to the wall. Nick is the only one to join me. Almost everyone else follows Grant and his cast to the bench. A couple of kids trail Ryan to the basketball court. From across the playground, I watch Thermos look at them for a second. Then she jogs over to Nick and me.

"Want to play Antidisestablishmentarianism?" she asks. It's like H-O-R-S-E, but longer.

"Want to see my coupon?" I pull it out of my pocket to show them. It's crumpled and dog-eared, and in the bright sunlight of the playground it doesn't look quite as impressive as I'd pictured in my head.

"I guess it's not that big a deal." I smooth it against my leg.

"I think it's cool," Thermos says. "What are you going to buy with it?"

I shrug. I almost don't want to buy anything because then I won't have the coupon anymore.

"If we come up with a three-way costume," Nick says, "you could use it to buy your part."

Thermos leaves her basketball on the wood chips and starts climbing the rock wall. Nick grabs a couple of handgrips and hangs. I lean back against the wall as Ava walks over to us.

"Hi, Nick."

Nick mumbles something that sounds like *Harrowava*. Ava giggles. I don't think she knows what he said either. Nick climbs up to the top of the wall where Thermos is. They both look down at Ava and me.

Then we all wait around, as silent as the falling leaves. Nick usually does the talking when other kids join our group. I don't know what's wrong with him today.

"Hey, Ava," I say. "Want to see my coupon?"

I hold it out, and Ava looks it over. She asks what I'm going to be for Halloween.

"We're doing a three-way costume." I point to my chest, then at Nick and Thermos, still watching us silently from the top of the rock wall. "If we can think of a three-way costume. There's got to be something that would be perfect for us," I say.

"How about the Three Musketeers?" Ava suggests.

"Maybe," I say.

"Too serious," says Thermos.

Nick mumbles something that sounds like *eyewipe blanket*.

"What about a sandwich?" Ava suggests. "Two

slices of bread and a piece of baloney?" Ava tilts her head, thinking. "Though it might be hard to walk unless you keep the pieces separate."

Nick climbs down from the rock wall. He's looking at Ava like he can't believe she suggested a sandwich. *"Sandwiches armifavorg,"* he mumbles.

I think Nick might be going crazy. I screw my face up at Thermos. She bulges her eyes and nods in a way that means *I think you're right.*

"Hey! How about the three bears?" Thermos shouts down from above us.

"Possibly," I say. It doesn't feel quite perfect.

"The three blind mice? The three little pigs? The three billy goats gruff?" Thermos rattles off her suggestions superfast. "The three grumpy socks?"

I crack up.

"What are the three grumpy socks?" Ava asks. "I've never heard of them."

"Thermos was joking," I explain. Nick nods his head, and Ava smiles, but she still looks confused.

"It would be a good kiddie story. Don't you

think?" Thermos grins. She swings her legs over the top of the rock wall and hangs there.

"Yeah," I agree. "They have to watch out for the big bad shoe."

"Oh, I get it," Ava says. But it doesn't seem like she does.

Then we all wait around not saying anything or doing anything again. We're like the four awkward lampposts. Then it hits me.

"What about the Three Stooges? When people open their doors, Nick could slap Thermos and Thermos could poke me in the eyes, and I could say, *'Woob-woob-woob!'*"

"I love it!" Thermos jumps down from the top of the wall.

"I think I've heard of the Three Stooges," Ava says. "Do you like them?" she asks Nick.

He nods his head really fast. *Sheesh.* I'd say the cat's got his tongue, but Nick is allergic to cats. I didn't think he'd ever get close enough to a cat to let it get his tongue.

Lunch recess is almost over, so we all start

walking back to the fifth-grade entrance, but Ava stops to tie her shoes.

"Will somebody wait for me?" she asks.

Nick, Thermos, and I look at one another. Neither of them says anything. Thermos stares longingly at the empty basketball area and I know she wants to shoot a few more baskets before recess ends. Nick stares at the grass. I figure he wouldn't want to walk with Ava when he can't even talk to her, so I say, "I will."

"Oh." Ava looks a bit surprised. "Okay."

Thermos shakes her head at me and Nick gets a funny expression on his face, but they walk off together leaving Ava and me alone.

When Ava finishes tying her shoes, we start walking again.

"Who's your favorite comedian?" I ask her.

"I don't know any comedians," she says.

"What? That's crazy! What about your friends? Who do they like?"

"I don't know," she says. "Maybe . . ." Ava looks

at me sideways. "Maybe you and Nick could tell Hannah and me about some of your favorite comedians after school someday."

I reach back and pat my lucky coupon because it's totally working. Ava is treating me like I'm any normal kid. The kind of kid you could hang out with. I'm about to say, "Sure," when barfsaster strikes.

"Louie Burger has a girlfriend! Louie's in love! Hey, loveburgers!" Ryan starts making kissy faces at me and Ava, and a bunch of kids laugh. My cheeks flame up. I turn to Ava, ready to apologize for Ryan being such a jerk, but she's gone. She's raced ahead of me and is already back with her friends by the four-square area.

As I speed walk to Nick and Thermos at the basketball court, Ryan follows me, making kissing sounds the whole way.

"Stop it," Nick snaps at Ryan.

"I was just kidding," Ryan says, but he does stop. "Let's go," he says to his friends. They are all watching Thermos sink three-pointer after three-pointer. It's as if they don't hear him. Ryan walks off alone.

"Thanks," I whisper to Nick.

Nick shrugs. "Whatever."

"Are you mad at me? What did I do?"

Nick shrugs again. He looks over at Ava and her friends sitting on the bench by the door. "Nothing. You didn't do anything."

o o o

After lunch, as my class walks down the hall to gym, "The Imperial Death March" plays in my head. There is no way I can dance with Ava in front of my entire class. That'll be the final chapter in Ryan's Book of Loveburger. I'll never hear the end of it. My status is hanging in the balance. It doesn't seem like anyone even remembers that I was on *Lou Lafferman.* One wrong move and I'm back to class B.U.R.P.

Each step I take down the hallway brings me closer and closer to my doom. We pass the water fountain and the art room. We pass the cafeteria and the resource center. It's only twenty-five steps more until I get to gym.

There must be some way to avoid dancing with Ava. Maybe Mr. Lamb will let me change partners. But I've never heard of Mr. Lamb changing anyone's partner before. I've never heard of Mr. Lamb doing anything nice for anyone. Ever.

Five more steps to go. My eyes scramble around looking for something that might help me. The only thing I see is a poster of a kitten that says "Hang in there." Not helpful.

We file into the gym and sit down on the blue line. Mr. Lamb demonstrates a do-si-do and then he tells us to find our partners. I don't know what comes over me, but when I stand up I grab my stomach, double over, and shout, "Oh no, I think I have stomach flu!"

Mr. Lamb peers into my face. "You sure?"

I nod my head and moan. I don't think he believes me, but since I did recently throw up on national television, he's not taking any chances.

"Okay," he says. "Go to the nurse's office."

I keep a sick expression on my face as I walk out the door and down the hall. When I turn the corner, I stand up straight and reach into my pocket to touch the coupon. Whew! That was a close one, and I can't let it happen again. If I want everyone to like me, I've got to make them laugh, not let them laugh at me!

THE SECRET OF BUMPS

After school, Nick, Thermos, and I hang out in the new location of Louie's Laff Shack. Louie's Laff Shack is my very own comedy club and it used to be located in my closet. Don't ask. I have a huge closet even though my bedroom is smaller than a Tonka truck. A little while ago, Thermos and I cleaned out my family's garage, which was more fun than you'd think, and I decided to move my club outside to the right half of the garage and add stadium seating. Right now stadium seating is three folding chairs. The left half of the garage is my dad's art studio work space. He's a junk artist. That's a real thing. People will actually buy junk if you glue two pieces of it together and call it art.

We're sitting on my stage eating our after-school snacks, Fluffernutters for Thermos and me, peanut butter and pickles for Nick. Ruby and my dad are on the other side of the garage going through boxes of our old Halloween decorations and eating whatever leftover Halloween candy they find from last year. The recycled recycling bins my dad has been working on are shoved way into the corner, and the Halloween stuff has taken over. Halloween obviously has nothing to do with junk art, but I don't want to bring that up. My dad takes Halloween very, very seriously.

"Do these bat wings look droopy to you guys?" My father holds up a rubber bat whose wings hang like wet socks.

"Uh, sort of," I say.

He twists his lips and wrinkles his nose and puts twelve bats at the far end of his large worktable. "That will be the maybe pile," he tells Ruby.

"Oh no!" Dad pulls a jumble of bones from the decoration box. "The skeletons are tangled."

"What did the skeleton say when he walked into the coffee shop?" I ask him.

"I hope it was something about how to untangle this mess." My father gives one of the kneecaps a tug and it pops off.

"Nope," I tell him, as Ruby chases the bone rolling across the floor. "He said, 'Give me a cappuccino and a mop.'"

Ruby laughs. "I get it," she says, finally stopping the kneecap with her foot. "Because he wants to get a job there!"

Now Nick and Thermos laugh. "Almost," I tell Ruby, shaking my head at her. "Think about what will happen after he drinks his coffee."

Ruby stares at the skeleton for a long time, then she says, "Oooh! He's going to use the mop for hair!"

Thermos pops the last bite of her Fluffernutter in her mouth and says, with her mouth full, "No more joking around. We've got to work on our costumes!"

"You could be unicorns!" Ruby says. "Guess what I'm going to be?"

"A unicorn," I say. "You already told me."

"Yeah, but what kind of unicorn?"

"Dad," I say, and I point to Ruby. "Could you help us out here? We're trying to work on our costumes."

"Ruby!" my father calls to Ruby from the top of a ladder. "You're just the girl I need. Will you catch these ghosts as they fly down from the sky?"

Ruby runs away from my dad and grabs a tiny gray bag from a shelf in the corner of the garage.

"Look! I found it! I've been looking for it since a million years ago." She opens the bag and pulls out our video camera. The one she used to record my performance at the Barker Back-to-School Bonanza talent show.

"Louie, I can make another video of you!"

"Not now, Ruby. We've got to work on our costumes. We've got a good idea, but we have to practice if we want it to be barftastic. I want to have the coolest costume in the whole school."

"As long as we like it, who cares?" Nick says.

"Yeah," Thermos agrees. "Everybody likes different kinds of costumes anyway."

That may be true, but I still want to have the coolest costume. Because if I have a cool costume, then people might think I'm cool. And if they think I'm cool, they won't think I'm a B.U.R.P.

I grab my Three Stooges bobbleheads from my bobblehead shelf and put them on the stage between us. "First, we have to decide who's who. Thermos, you should be Larry since you have the longest hair. Nick, you be Moe, and I'll be Curly. Dad, can I get a buzz cut?"

Ruby steps up onto my stage and brings the camera really close to the bobbleheads.

"Dad!" I shout. "Come on! We're trying to work."

"Sorry, Louie! I got distracted." My father climbs down from his ladder, takes Ruby by the hand, and leads her back to his side of the garage. "I really need your help, Ruby. I want our house to be the most popular house in the neighborhood."

"If you want to be the most popular, I'll tell you

the secret." Ari walks into the garage. She doesn't hang out here that much. She prefers to stay inside and have the entire house to herself. Ever since she started middle school, Ari acts like privacy is the most important thing in the world. As her younger brother, I usually feel it is my duty to tease her about that, or one of the other million weird things about her, but I don't just now. Her words have intrigued me. The secret to being popular?

"Okay," I tell her. "Spill it."

Ari studies me and then shifts her hip to one side, resting her hand against it. "First, I'll tell Dad. His is easier. If you want to be the most popular house on Halloween, there is only one way. Candy. It's got to be the good kind, and it's got to be full-size. Raisins, pretzels, and granola bars don't cut it, even if they've got Halloween wrappers."

My father's face falls and he shakes his head. "There's no way your mom will let me pass out full-size candy bars. They're too unhealthy. I'm doomed."

"Unicorns like raisins." Ruby puts one arm around my father's shoulder. Her other arm is now pointing the camera at Ari.

I feel like I should say something to cheer my dad up as well, but I really want to know that secret. Now. Before Ari changes her mind. I didn't know there was actually a secret to being popular. "Okay, okay, so Dad will never be popular. But what about me?"

Ari cracks her knuckles like this is going to be hard work. She flips one of the folding chairs around and sits on it backward. "Okay, you three, listen up."

"Not me." Thermos shakes her head. "Who cares about being popular."

"Yeah," says Nick. "I'm happy with the friends I have."

"Don't listen to them," I tell Ari. "Tell us."

"Okay," she says. "There are three ways to be popular." She looks me up and down. "But only the third one will work for you. That's not completely an insult by the way. The first way is by being mean. Everyone's afraid of you, so everyone tries to be on your good side. You're popular, but no one actually likes you."

"That's Ryan Rakefield," Nick says.

"I don't know," I say, remembering the Corn Maze. "His friends like him."

"Anyway," Ari says, giving us a teacherly look like she's going to send us to the office if we interrupt her again. I want to tell her she's not the boss of us, but she hasn't finished revealing the secret yet, so I keep my mouth shut. "The second way is by being one of those super-nice, great-personality kids that everyone loves."

"That's you!" Thermos points at Nick.

He blushes. "I don't think I'm . . ."

"Yep," I say. "That's you. What's the third way?"

"The third way is bumps." Ari shrugs one shoulder as if she's said something completely obvious.

"Bumps?" I ask.

"Like pimples?" Thermos wrinkles her nose.

"Like goose bumps?" Nick sits up.

"Popularity bumps," Ari explains. "Certain

things, like getting a new dog, or having a birthday party, or breaking your leg, give your popularity a bump. For a few days, or sometimes even a few weeks afterward, everyone wants to be around you and you're more popular than you used to be."

"That's like Grant," I say. "He broke his arm and everyone's been following him around asking him how it happened and begging to sign his cast."

"Exactly!" Ari nods at me like I'm a good student. "I bet you got a bump when you were on TV."

I nod my head slowly because I got one, but it might be over.

"I bet it didn't last, right?" Ari points her finger at me and I nod again. "Don't take it personally. That's the way the bumps work. You go up, you go down."

"So if you want to stay popular," I say, "you have to keep getting bumps."

Nick laughs. "That's impossible. You can't break your arm or have a birthday or be on TV every week."

"And who wants everyone to like you because you broke your arm? They're not real friends if that's what they care about," Thermos adds.

I act like I agree with what Nick and Thermos are saying, but inside I know they can only afford to say those kinds of things because they've never been a B.U.R.P.

Ari stands up and turns back to our father. "The only reason I came out here was to ask if I could ride my bike to Madison's house. I'll be home by dinner. Oh, and the recycling company called. They asked you to call them back as soon as possible."

"Sure. Yeah. Thanks," my dad says absentmindedly as he piles our fake tombstones in a corner of the garage. Most of them are chipped. "Healthy treats and decrepit decorations. Things are not looking good for the Burger Halloween."

I watch Dad finger our faded and fraying pumpkin banner, and have to agree with him. Nick, Thermos, and I spend the rest of the afternoon practicing our Three Stooges moves while Ruby acts like she's our director. It takes about an hour to get our slap fest down to a science.

○ ○ ○

After dinner, I head back out to the Laff Shack and lie down in the middle of my stage. I like to be alone in there. It's a good place to think. Ari's popularity secret has been buzzing around my brain like a bee that drank twelve sugary sodas.

Nick and Thermos thought bumps were a silly idea, but when I had my viewer-video bump, most kids ignored Ryan's teasing. The further I get away from the bump, the more they laugh at me again. If I could get another bump, and then another, maybe the teasing would go away. Permanently.

The problem is I have no idea what could bump me. I list the cool things that have happened to me lately:

1. *A video of me barfing at the fifth-grade talent show was featured on my favorite late-night talk show. That bump's already come and gone.*

2. *The local Halloween store gave me a 20-percent-off coupon. I tried to get a bump from that, but no one seemed to care.*

3. *Uh. Um.*

4. *I believe the expression that applies here is: I got nothin'.*

So if nothing has happened that can give me a bump, maybe I can make something happen. I wonder how much it would hurt to break my leg, but decide I'm too chicken to try. I grab my microphone. Sometimes doing a stand-up routine is the only way to figure stuff out.

"What's the deal with Halloween? Three hundred and sixty-four days of the year grownups tell kids not to take candy from strangers. Then on Halloween they tell us to hit up as many strangers as possible. Three hundred and sixty-four days of the year grownups check for monsters under our beds, won't let us see horror movies, and tell us everything in the world is safe and cozy. Then on Halloween they try to scare the patooties out of us. Three hundred and sixty-four days of the year grownups tell us we should 'be ourselves.' Then on Halloween, they tell us to dress up in costume."

I wonder if costumes are disguises, or if they reveal our true, secret selves. Have you ever noticed how every school has one teacher who always dresses like the Wicked Witch of the West? She's also the one who sometimes makes her class miss recess because "we are so engaged in learning!" My dad always dresses as an artist, and did so even before he lost his job as a vice president. Last year he was van Gogh with a bloody ear hanging off the side of his head. My mother always dresses as Super Mom, in a superhero costume with a cape and a big *M* on her chest. In real life she's a gym teacher.

I sit down on the side of my stage and look up at my new wall of comedy, filled with posters of my favorite comedians. Tonight my eyes lock on Charlie Chaplin. *He* wore a costume. In most of his movies, he dressed as the tramp, a poor, well-meaning guy who was often misunderstood. Maybe that's how he felt inside. I can relate.

Charlie started as a nobody and then became the biggest comedian and most well-known guy in the entire world. By being funny.

I think about Charlie's funniest bits: dancing with a dog's leash tied around his waist like a belt, being chased up and down in an elevator, fighting with a police officer. Maybe that's the key. Being funny. I'm wondering what I could do that my classmates would think was funny, when I hear a knock on the side door of the garage.

"Come in."

My mom opens the door and pokes her head through the crack. "Time to get ready for bed."

I walk back to the house with her, my shoulders shivering because the night is chilly. Mom puts her arm around me to warm me up and hands me an envelope. "This came in the mail for you today."

"Thanks." I open it, but it's too dark to read it outside.

"Guess what?" my mom says. Her voice makes it sound like it's something super exciting.

"Lou Lafferman called? He wants me on the show?"

She tousles my hair. "Mr. Lamb called. He invited me to be on the district's physical education task force! It's a huge honor for a first-year teacher. He said he admires my commitment to fun fitness."

It's weird to see my mom so happy about gym, but it also makes me smile. "Um, congratulations," I say.

As we walk past our basketball hoop, she jumps up and lets her fingers brush the net. "You know what, Louie? I love my job. I wasn't sure how I would feel when I first went back to work this fall, but I'm really glad I did. Is it strange having Dad home all the time instead of me?"

I purse my lips and think. "It's different, but not bad. You always had a snack ready for us when we got home, but he lets us have more cookies. I like both ways."

My mom laughs. "It doesn't sound too terrible."

When we get inside, I finally check out the letter my mom gave me. It's an invitation to Nick's Spooky Halloween Birthday Bash, two days before Halloween. I know Nick's party is going to be a lot of fun, but a little voice in my head is also pointing out that Nick is going to get a popularity bump from this. Ari wasn't clear about specifics, but I don't think two kids can get a bump at the same time. As soon as Grant broke his arm, my video bump was gone. And I bet tomorrow, Grant's broken-arm bump will be gone because everyone will want to know more about Nick's birthday party.

I leave my shoes in the cubby next to the door and slide-walk down the hallway to my bedroom in my socks. When I get there, I hang Nick's invitation on my bulletin board and flop down onto my bed. The thing is: *I* wanted a bump.

MAKE 'EM LAUGH

Thursday morning, I spring out of bed, even before my dad wakes me up. That never happens. Usually he has to come back into my room four or five times and tickle my feet, stick a feather in my ear, steal my covers, and spray my face with water. But not today. Today I want to go to school and make people laugh.

I get dressed, but instead of wearing one of my regular shirts, I grab my favorite joke book and a plain white undershirt from my underwear drawer. I write a joke across the chest. Then I race to the Laff Shack and gather up my collection of classic comedian bobbleheads: Charlie Chaplin, Laurel and Hardy, Buster Keaton, the Marx

Brothers, and the Three Stooges. I put them in a large shoe box. They will be hard to carry around, but it will be worth it when everyone asks about them.

People will probably think the bobbleheads are so cool, they will want to know more about them. So I'll start an old-timey comedy club at recess. Then I will invite everyone over to my house after school to watch movies. I'll be elected president of the club, of course, and Nick and Thermos will be my co-presidents. Ryan Rakefield will finally admit that he's been wrong about me since first grade. He'll wish he could take all the years of teasing back, and he'll beg to be in my club. I tuck my coupon into my back pocket and leave for school.

When Ruby and I meet Nick and Henry at the foot of my driveway, the first thing Nick and I do is the Barf Brothers' Secret Handshake. (Well, actually, it's the second thing because first I have to put down the bobbleheads. They are really heavy.) The Barf Brothers' Secret Handshake has been our special greeting ever since the time we were in second grade and we both threw up after eating an entire meat-lover's pizza at a sleepover.

"You know what, Henry?" Ruby rubs her chin like she's a professor. "We need a handshake."

"Yeah." Henry rubs his chin, too.

"It will be named the Unicorn Magic Headshake Handshake." Ruby lowers her head and then paws her right foot at the ground like a horse. She whinnies, tosses her imaginary unicorn horn, and rears back, waving her two fists at Henry like they are hooves. "Try it!"

I scan up and down our street but don't see anyone but us, so Nick and I give it a try, too. It's nowhere near as good as the Barf Brothers' Secret Handshake, but Ruby and Henry don't seem to mind. They skip off ahead, still acting like unicorns. As soon as they are gone, Nick and I both start talking at the same time.

"Do you think everyone will like my bobbleheads?" I ask as Nick says, "Did you get my invitation?"

"Wait, what?" Nick shakes his head.

"My bobbleheads." I pick the box back up and slide the lid off center so Nick can see inside. We start walking. "I thought I'd bring them to school to show people. Because they're funny."

"Oh." Nick shrugs his shoulders like he doesn't quite get it. "But did you read my invitation?" he asks. "Did you see we're doing a haunted house this year? We're going to do that game where you close your eyes and have to reach your hand into bowls of eyeballs, brains, and guts. We're going to tell ghost stories, and we're going to do a blindfold walk in my basement. Henry and my dad are going to grab people's ankles and put icy fingers on the backs of their necks. It's going to be terrifying and awesome!"

"Yeah. I can't wait," I say, and nod at Nick. Then I shift my box around a bit because my arms are starting to get tired. "So, you'll probably get a birthday bump."

"I guess." Nick reaches into my box and taps Buster's head. Buster nods like he's agreeing the bump is going to be barfgantic.

"I hadn't thought about it," Nick adds.

"That's what I figured." We cross the street with the crossing guard. Ruby and Henry are already way ahead of us, in the first-grade area, teaching everyone the Unicorn Magic Headshake Handshake. "You probably wouldn't even care if someone else got a bump today instead of you, right?"

Nick pauses for a minute, studies me, then says, "I guess not, but do you want to come over the day before my party and help set everything up? My mom said I was allowed to invite you and Thermos. It'll be like two parties in a row because we'll have to practice everything to make sure it works."

"Sure. That sounds awesome."

As we get closer to Barker Elementary School, I hold my breath and concentrate on my coupon for luck. I want today's bump.

"Nick," Grant shouts as Nick and I finish crossing the street and step onto the blacktop. "I got your invitation!"

When I finally exhale, Nick and I are surrounded

by everyone Nick invited to his party. The crowd is huge. He must have invited the whole grade. I edge myself to the outside of the crowd. People are jostling my bobblehead box and I don't want it to get crushed.

"Are you going to do that thing with the eyeballs?" Mason asks Nick. A few orange leaves flutter down from the oak tree next to our school and Nick jumps up and catches them.

"Yep," he says.

"Do we get to wear our costumes?" Ava asks. "Hannah and I are going to be two peas in a pod."

Nick smiles at his shoes and nods. Then he whispers something I can barely make out. It sounds like *Darfintly cobstupes.*

Other kids start asking Nick questions about his party, but he doesn't even notice them. Ava and Hannah have walked away whispering and Nick is watching their backs. Grant elbows Owen and points at Nick. They both make kissy faces. Mason sees them and he joins in. *Love teasing.* I have to save Nick.

"Hey!" I say loudly. "Does anyone want to see my classic comedians bobblehead collection?"

A couple of kids turn away from the crowd and look at me. It's showtime.

"Classic comedians?" Grant asks.

I pick up the little statues of Groucho, Harpo, and Chico Marx, each with its giant head attached to springs. I tap them and they nod in different rhythms. "I'm Groucho Marx," I say in my best Groucho imitation. "My brother here thinks he's a chicken. We don't talk him out of it because we need the eggs."

"Ha!" Owen says, stepping over and tapping Groucho's head.

"Can I see one?" Grant asks, as a couple more kids turn around.

"Sure." I hand him Harpo Marx, then pick up another statue, feeling a tiny pang of worry as Grant balances the figurine on his cast, then taps its head with a little too much force. The bobbleheads are fragile. I don't want them to get broken.

But I don't want to be a B.U.R.P. either.

"Where did you find so many old-fashioned characters?" Hannah speaks right in my ear, and I jump the way you jump when your grandma walks into your dressing room during back-to-school shopping and you are wearing nothing but an old pair of Spider-Man underpants that you never wear anymore but that was the only clean pair left. And the saleslady sees everything.

Not that that actually happened. *Really.*

Startled, I take a step back. I didn't realize Ava and Hannah had returned. Nick, now standing behind Ava, looks upset. I offer him a bobblehead, but he shakes his head.

"I ordered them online," I tell Hannah, offering her the bobblehead instead.

"Can I borrow this one?" Grant asks. "You have so many."

My skin squirms. I don't want to give away a bobblehead, even though I know it's not forever. But I want Grant to like them. And me.

"Uh, for how long?" I ask.

"I'm here!" Ryan Rakefield dribbles his basketball as he walks over to us from the bus drop-off. Behind him, Thermos races straight to the basketball hoops to get some shots in before the boys monopolize the court.

"It's time for some b-ball." Ryan pretends to shoot a basket.

Nobody looks up at him because they are still playing with my bobbleheads.

"What's going on?" Ryan barges into the center of the group and looks around. "Cool," he says to Grant. "What are those?" He puts his finger on Groucho's head and tilts it way, way back. It looks like it's about to snap off.

"Louie brought them," Grant explains. "They're old comedians."

Ryan looks at me, then looks around at all the kids checking out my bobbleheads. He presses his finger harder.

"Careful!" I shout. I can't help myself. I believe the expression for what is about to happen is: *Off with his bobblehead.*

"Sorry!" Ryan uses a sweet voice and his face

actually looks sorry. But the hairs on my arm stand up anyway. There is no way he's sincere.

"I didn't mean to hurt your *doll*," he says.

I look around the group, my heart beating hard. Bobbleheads aren't dolls. But Grant and Owen toss the bobbleheads back in the box as if they are as hot as a rubber chicken you accidentally left sitting in the middle of the road on a hot summer day.

Oh no. Is a rubber chicken a doll?

I scramble to put the lid on the box. The word *doll* is like poison, and now every boy is giving me a strange look. I can't get the lid to line up and I stumble forward, my right hand landing on Harpo with a weird crunch. I look down with a sick feeling growing in my stomach. Harpo's been decapitated.

Ryan holds up his basketball. "Who's in?"

Owen and James stand up.

"Wait!" I stand up, too. They can't go yet. What about my bobblehead impressions? What about my joke shirt? I unzip my sweatshirt and point to the words on my chest.

Hannah tilts her head to the side and wrinkles her nose. "What do you call a pip that knows karate? What's a pip?"

"Not a pip!" I pull my shirt away from my chest and try to read it upside down. "Pig! What do you call a *pig* that knows karate? A pork chop."

"That doesn't look like pig," Hannah says. She tugs on Ava's sleeve. "Doesn't that say pip?"

Ava nods. "It sort of looks like pip," she says. "Sorry."

"That definitely says pip," James says.

"Let's go pip some baskets," Ryan says, laughing. "Oops, I mean shoot."

Owen and James follow him to the basketball court as I zip my sweatshirt back up. Most of the kids that were checking out my bobbleheads start to walk away. "Let's go pip four square," I hear someone say.

Soon, only Grant and a couple of others are left. With his cast, Grant can't play basketball or four square. He scratches around the edge of the plaster, then says to Nick, "You should add witch fingers to your blindfold walk. You could have someone scratch people's arms as they walk by."

Nick trails his fingers down his forearm, considering. Then he shivers. "Good idea!"

Grant and Nick brainstorm more ideas. Hannah and Ava join in, and before long I'm standing on the edge of the crowd again. I play with my zipper, then kick my bobblehead box. It doesn't matter anyway. Harpo is already broken.

THE PERFECT BUMP

After lunch, Mrs. Adler has a big smile on her face when we return to class.

"It's only two weeks and a day until Halloween," she tells us as we file back to our desks. "Guess what that means?"

"It's time for everyone to choose me to lead the Halloween parade." Ryan stands up on his chair and takes a bow.

"Feet on the floor, Mr. Rakefield!" For once, Mrs. Adler does not look amused at Ryan's shtick. I smile on the inside, but also on the outside, because I have an idea. A way I could maybe, finally, beat Ryan Rakefield.

"I know most of you already know this, but for the benefit of any new students"—Mrs. Adler winks at Thermos—"I'm going to explain how we celebrate Halloween here. We don't mess around.

"On Halloween, students change into their costumes at lunchtime. After lunch, we have the annual Barker Elementary School Halloween Parade. Then we gather in the gym for an all-school sing-along followed by our class party. The day before Halloween, each class will choose one student to be marshal and lead them in the parade. Out of those students, the principal will choose one to be the grand marshal, who will walk at the head of the entire school."

When she says those words, my feet get tingly because *that* is it, the way to beat Ryan. If I can get my class to elect me class marshal, and get the principal to pick me as grand marshal, and if I have a costume that's so memorable no one can stop thinking about it, and the local news puts me in the paper like last year's marshal, then I'm sure to get a popularity bump so big Ryan will never be able to tease me again. I believe that the expression that applies here is: *Easy as pie.*

Ryan Rakefield raises his hand.

"I don't want anyone to volunteer right now," Mrs. Adler says. "Think it over, discuss it with your parents tonight, and you can let me know tomorrow. Okay, let's line up for gym."

As we walk down the hallway, my thoughts swirl with possibilities. I'm going to come up with the perfect front-of-the-parade costume. It'll be funny, but cool. When people see it, they will instantly be able to imagine me leading our class. And when the principal sees it, he will know right away that I'm the only kid who could possibly do a decent job as grand marshal. Everyone will be so impressed with the way I lead the parade that the image of me as the coolest kid in fifth grade will be etched into their brains. And the rule of Ryan Rakefield will come to an end.

I'm so lost in my daydreams, I don't notice that my class has stopped walking, and I slam right into the back of the person in front of me.

"Watch it!" Ryan Rakefield spins around and gives me a look that's half evil eye, half maniacal smile. "Don't want you to hurt yourself; then you won't be able to dance with your *true love*."

Beads of sweat instantly pop out on my forehead. If there is one thing that could end my dream of beating Ryan, it's the major popularity sinkhole that comes from being a D.O.L.T.: Direct Object of Love Teasing. Everyone loves to join in love teasing. It could go viral faster than my video.

I tilt my head to the side and peer up at the front of the line. We're waiting in the hallway because the class before us hasn't been picked up from gym yet. I see their teacher at the end of the connecting hallway. I only have a few seconds before he gets here. A few measly seconds that could change the rest of my life.

Then I get a brilliant idea. I rush to the front of the line and tell Mrs. Adler that I was supposed to go to the doctor's office today, and I forgot to give her my note. After she drops the class off, we go back to the classroom and I pretend to look through my backpack and folders for about five minutes until she tells me that I can go to the office without the note. I wait in the office for twenty minutes until the secretary finally asks if she should call someone. I smack myself on the forehead and say, "My mistake! I forgot. My appointment is *next* Thursday."

I return to my locker, put my things away, and head back to gym. When I get there, gym is over. Perfect.

"Burger, where were you?" Mr. Lamb asks.

"I thought I had a doctor's appointment," I say.

He frowns at me. "Get in line. Ask Jamal to show you what you missed."

I walk to the end of the line, passing Ryan on the way. He's got a red mark on his forehead, like he bumped it on something. I wonder if Thermos did that to him.

"You missed Jamal demonstrating how to swing his partner," Ryan says. "He's a reg'lar cowboy. Mr. Lamb wants him to enter a country-dance competition."

That sounds like nice stuff to me, but the tone of Ryan's voice doesn't sound complimentary. When I look over at Jamal, he's pretending not to hear. I'm not sure if I should feel bad for him, or relieved that Ryan isn't teasing me. It's confusing.

I slip to the back of the line and try to keep a low profile as we walk to our room. The class-marshal election is in two weeks. If I can avoid the teasing until then, I might have a chance to win.

MARSHAL MADNESS

The next day, I have to sit through morning announcements, writers' workshop, math groups, and science before Mrs. Adler finally asks everyone who wants to run for class marshal to raise their hands. My hand shoots up into the air and I look around the room to check out my competition. Ryan Rakefield's got his hand raised. He's staring at Mrs. Adler like he doesn't even care if anyone else has their hand raised. Like it won't even matter because he's so sure to win. Violet VanDeusen has her hand raised, too. She's got her arm stretched out so straight and so high, it's like she's trying to touch the ceiling. It's as if she's thinking, *See? See how high I can raise my hand?*

I look at my own raised hand, elbow bent, fingers curved. Then I look around the rest of the room to see if anyone else is throwing their costume into the ring. When I lock eyes with Nick, his jaw drops in disbelief.

"Okay," says Mrs. Adler. "Three candidates. Ryan, Violet, and Louie, please see me after school and I will give you a list of rules and expectations for you to share with your families. Now, everyone to the cafeteria, it's time for lunch."

Nick, Thermos, and I sit at our usual spot at the end of Mrs. Adler's first table in the cafeteria, and I unpack my Fluffernutter, my apple, and my vanilla yogurt. I take a big spoonful of yogurt and Nick bulges his eyes at me.

"Why would you volunteer to be class marshal?" He unpacks his ham-and-cheese sub, chips, and carrot sticks, but doesn't take a bite. "How can you eat right now?"

"I'm hungry. What's the big deal?" I take my first bite of Fluffernutter and lick the bits of extra fluff from the corners of my mouth.

"If you win class marshal, you can't walk with Thermos and me in the parade. What's the point of having a three-way costume if we're not going to be walking together?"

I stop chewing and think. I guess I forgot about the whole three-way-costume thing when I was imagining being class marshal. It really doesn't work to lead the parade in one third of a costume. "You're right. I'll walk with you guys on Halloween and do a separate costume for being marshal. I can't do a three-way costume for the parade."

Nick pushes away his sandwich, and Thermos takes a big slurp of chicken noodle soup. "Why do you even want to be class marshal anyway?" she asks. "It seems more like a punishment than a reward. The kid who wins doesn't get to walk with her friends. What good is that?"

"Yeah," Nick agrees. "Besides, what are Thermos and I supposed to do during the parade? Be the *Two* Stooges? If you run for marshal I'm not doing a three-way costume."

"You guys don't get it." I wave my spoon in the

air for emphasis. "The kid who wins is *chosen*. It's proof that everyone in the class thinks he's cool. That everyone likes him."

"How could that be true?" Nick asks. "Ryan has won every year since first grade. Usually because he buys everyone candy and toys and threatens to beat them up if they don't choose him."

"Yeah," Thermos says. "This is my first year here, and even I can tell this whole thing isn't about who would do the best job as marshal. It's a popularity contest."

"Exactly!" I throw my hands up in the air. Finally someone gets it.

Nick and Thermos exchange strange looks.

"Are you sure you wouldn't rather drop out and march with Thermos and me?" Nick peers at me hopefully.

"This is my chance to become a new Louie," I explain.

"I like the old Louie," Thermos says, shrugging. "But if you want us to help you, we will." She gives Nick a look. "Right?"

He purses his lips. "If we can. Ryan fights dirty, and I bet most of the girls will want to vote for Violet."

"We'll figure something out. That's what friends are for." Thermos takes a spoonful of soup and slurps up a noodle.

"Thanks!" Nick still isn't smiling though, so I add, "Hey, who would win a wrestling match, Jell-O or carrot sticks?"

Nick looks at me for a second, then he smiles reluctantly. "Jell-O," he finally says. "Any time the carrot tried to attack, he'd bounce right off."

"Unless," Thermos counters, "the carrot stick comes in at the right angle." She does a sideways chop with her hands. "Jell-O cubes!"

At that moment, Ryan stands up between Mrs. Adler's two tables and taps a spoon against his chocolate milk carton. It doesn't make a loud clinking sound the way it does when people tap their glass in the movies, but everyone still quiets down and pays attention to him.

"I'd like you to know that if I'm elected

marshal, I will bring in glow sticks for everyone to wear during the parade."

A bunch of kids nod and say, "Cool," and my stomach sinks because there is no way I can buy tons of stuff for my class. There has got to be some other way to win. I stand up and say, "I'd like everyone to know that if I'm elected marshal, I will write you your own personal joke to go with your costume! Here's a bonus joke: What did one glow stick say to the other glow stick?"

Ryan smiles. "You light up my life."

"Nope," I say, even though that was one of my possible punch lines. I don't want to give him the satisfaction of stepping on my joke.

"Way to glow!" Ryan jabs his fist in the air.

"Nope." I shake my head even though that was my second possible punch line and now I only have one left. I decide to shout it out before Ryan beats me to it. "Here we—"

"Glow again!" he finishes. "By the way, did I mention that not only would I be passing out glow sticks, I've also got glow necklaces and bracelets!"

Violet stands up. "I'm glad you both brought up glow sticks. Halloween safety is an important concern. Trick-or-treaters should wear reflective clothing so cars can see them. If you elect me, I will teach you many important Halloween safety tips."

"I can't wait," Ryan says sarcastically.

Violet doesn't seem to understand his tone. "You will have to," she says. "I will not pass out my tip sheet until tomorrow."

"Shhh!" The lunch dad, Mr. Pamprin, finally notices what's going on in the fifth-grade area and asks us to take our seats. "Lunch is over in five minutes. If you are finished, throw away your things and whisper quietly with your friends."

"What's the deal with school-lunch rules?" I plop back down between Nick and Thermos, shaking my head. "It was the principal's idea to stick four hundred kids in the same room at the same time. How do they expect the room to be quiet?"

"I don't know," Nick whispers.

Thermos grabs my arm, a serious look on her face. "Do you have enough jokes for everyone?"

"Yep," I say. "And I'm going to win." I reach into my back pocket and touch my coupon. "I can feel it in my bones."

On Saturday morning, it's time to get to work. If I'm going to win this election I've got a lot of stuff to do. First, I've got to come up with the perfect costume. Second, I've got to make killer posters. Third, I've got to write jokes for everyone in my class. And fourth, I have to get everyone to see me as a winner.

Hey, I never said it would be easy. But if I can get Ryan Rakefield off my back, it'll be worth it.

I grab myself a bowl of Fluff and apple slices to fuel my brain and head outside to the Laff Shack. Even though running for marshal isn't a joke, I know I'll do my best thinking in my comedy club. I do a little work on my routine first, to give my brain a warm-up. The second my hand wraps around the microphone, all my worries and doubts fade away.

"Did you ever notice that a lot of grownups complain about their jobs? I don't know about you, but I definitely don't want to feel that way when I'm grown up. But I'm pretty sure I've figured out a solution. There's one thing kids have that grownups don't.

"Recess!

"If grownups had recess, I bet they'd like their day a lot better. Imagine it. You'd go in for your checkup and the receptionist would say, 'Have a seat. Dr. Singh is doing the monkey bars. She'll be with you in a moment.' Later, she'd be in such a great mood you wouldn't have to get a shot.

"And how about librarians? I bet if they got to read books on the swings twice a day, they wouldn't be shushing everyone all the time.

"If you want to be happy, you should choose a job that's like recess all the time. For example, a paleontologist. That's kind of like playing in the sandbox."

After I do my recess bit a couple more times, I sit down with a pad of paper and a pen for brainstorming ideas about my costume. It's got to be the exact, perfect, front-of-the-parade costume. I start a list:

- o Barftastic Boy
- o A meat-lover's pizza
- o Lou Lafferman
- o Fireworks
- o Windshield wipers

Good costume ideas, but none of them feel exactly right. I look around the room and my eyes settle once again on my poster of Charlie Chaplin as the tramp. His tramp shoes are too big and his vest is too small. Everything about him is mismatched and wrong, exactly the way I feel whenever I have to deal with Ryan Rakefield.

Even though the tramp is an underdog, he is also the character that made Charlie Chaplin's

career. Everyone loved the tramp. He was the loser sometimes, but people still loved him, and they laughed *with* him. They cheered for him to succeed.

It's the perfect costume! I stand up and practice doing the tramp's funny shuffling walk around the edges of my stage. Every time I get to a corner, I skid on one ankle as I turn, exactly the way Charlie Chaplin did whenever his character was being chased in a movie. I picture myself leading the parade and skidding around the corners of the school. It will look great! No one has ever led the parade with so much style.

I head inside to get to work on my campaign posters, and almost fall over with shock when I get to the kitchen. Ruby is sitting at the table surrounded by poster boards, tubes of glitter, and markers.

"You can use this yarn for unicorn manes," Ari says, cutting a ball of orange yarn into strands and passing them to Ruby.

"What are you making?" I ask, even though I have a feeling I know the answer already.

"These are my poster-board boards so my class will choose me to lead the whole entire parade. Want to know what I'm going to be for Halloween?"

"A unicorn," I say. "I know."

"But what kind?"

"The kind with a lot of glitter, obviously." I brush some glitter off the kitchen table as Ruby dumps half a tube more onto her poster board.

"More people will choose you if you have lots

of sparklies." She offers the tube to me. "I'm being a loonicorn because that's my two favorite things."

"A loony-corn?" I don't have the heart to tell her that crazy and unicorns aren't two different things. I grab my poster boards from the bag my dad left next to the table. "Can you guys make some room here?" I point at the table, and Ari slides Ruby's stuff over so that a quarter of the table is clear for me.

"Gee, thanks." I set my first poster board down, and get to work penciling in my slogan. Once the letters look the way I want them, I go over them in black marker. I'm going to keep my posters black-and-white since most of Charlie's movies were black-and-white.

Vote for Louie!
He's a classic,
like Charlie!

I take my time on each letter, carefully sketching the special block caps that I learned how to do in art in third grade. I'm going to glue black-and-white photos of Charlie Chaplin around the edges. I'm biting the cap of my marker and considering whether or not to underline the word *classic* when I realize Ari is squinting one eye at my poster.

"What?" I put my hands on my hips and give her my death stare.

"Never mind," she says. "If I tell you, you'll get mad at me."

I fold my arms across my chest. "Now you have to tell me. And I'm going to get mad at you either way, so you might as well spit it out."

"Well . . ." Ari runs her hand along the edge of my poster. "Are you sure you want to be Charlie Chaplin? I mean, no one knows who he is. If you want to win you should be someone everyone's heard of, like Dracula or Superman or a banana or a sumo wrestler."

"Or a unicorn." Ruby nods her head in agreement with herself.

"But if I'm one of those things, then someone else will probably have the same costume," I tell them. "I want to be something no one at Barker has ever been before. And also, I want to be something that fits who I am."

"Me, too." Ruby nods again. "Nobody has ever been the same kind of unicorn as I'm going to be. I'm adding special addings to it." She glues even more orange yarn on to her poster.

Ari's face is filled with doubt. "I hear what you're saying, but I think it's risky. If people don't know who Charlie Chaplin is, and they don't understand about being a costume that represents who you are, then they aren't going to get your posters."

Ari does have a point.

But I have a solution.

I'll help them understand.

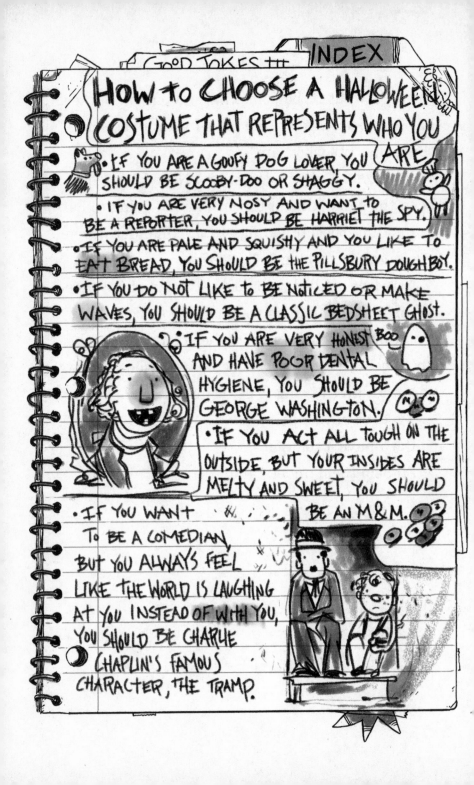

HOW to CHOOSE A HALLOWEEN COSTUME THAT REPRESENTS WHO YOU ARE

- IF YOU ARE A GOOFY DOG LOVER, YOU SHOULD BE SCOOBY-DOO OR SHAGGY.

- IF YOU ARE VERY NOSY AND WANT TO BE A REPORTER, YOU SHOULD BE HARRIET THE SPY.

- IF YOU ARE PALE AND SQUISHY AND YOU LIKE TO EAT BREAD, YOU SHOULD BE THE PILLSBURY DOUGHBOY.

- IF YOU DO NOT LIKE TO BE NOTICED OR MAKE WAVES, YOU SHOULD BE A CLASSIC BEDSHEET GHOST.

- IF YOU ARE VERY HONEST AND HAVE POOR DENTAL HYGIENE, YOU SHOULD BE GEORGE WASHINGTON.

BOO

- IF YOU ACT ALL TOUGH ON THE OUTSIDE, BUT YOUR INSIDES ARE MELTY AND SWEET, YOU SHOULD BE AN M&M.

- IF YOU WANT TO BE A COMEDIAN, BUT YOU ALWAYS FEEL LIKE THE WORLD IS LAUGHING AT YOU INSTEAD OF WITH YOU, YOU SHOULD BE CHARLIE CHAPLIN'S FAMOUS CHARACTER, THE TRAMP.

HOW TO BE A TREE

After lunch, I am about to clear my plate when my mother whisks it away from me and puts it in the sink.

I blink at her a couple of times. "You just cleared my plate for me," I tell her. "You never clear our plates. You always say that if you do it for us, it won't become automatic and clearing your plate should be automatic."

My mother sits back down next to me and smiles. "But sometimes a mom just wants to do something nice. Can't a mom do something nice?"

"Sure, I guess." Her smile grows bigger and I start to feel suspicious. "I've got a lot of math homework this weekend. You could do that for me, too, if you really want to be nice."

My mother raises an eyebrow at me, but she's not seriously upset. She knows my sense of humor. "Actually," she says, "I was hoping you'd do something nice for me."

"Okay. What?"

My mother hugs me, and then gets up from the table. "I'll let you know as soon as Nick and Theodora get here. I'll need all three of you."

My mother heads out to the backyard, and I gulp. I'm always happy to help my mom, but why does she need my friends? I'm starting to think I shouldn't have agreed so quickly. Besides, *I* need my friends. I want to go over my posters and my slogan with them and see if we can come up with any other campaign ideas. I'm going to have to get creative if I want to beat Ryan.

When Nick and Thermos arrive, we head to the backyard. My mother has spread a bunch of colored mats all over the grass. Ari and her friends and Ruby and Henry are already standing on them.

"Welcome to School Day Yoga!" My mother puts her hands together in front of her chest and bows to us as we walk over to three empty mats. "Thank you for being my test subjects. I want to convince the district to add yoga to the physical education curriculum, and I need to tweak my lessons before I present them to the committee."

"Wait a minute." I hold my hand up.

"Are you saying I have to take a gym class on the weekend?"

My mother winks at me. "It's your lucky day."

"I love yogurt!" Ruby stands on one foot and puts her hands together in front of her chest just like my mother.

I look back and forth at Nick and Thermos. "Sorry," I whisper. "I didn't know she was going to make us do this."

Thermos kicks off her shoes and straightens her shoulders. "I don't mind," she says. "I've always wanted to try yoga."

Nick takes his shoes off, too. "We used to do it at my preschool. I kind of like it."

My mother instructs us to take a deep breath and raise our hands to the sky. I'm full of questions I want to ask my friends, but I do as she says, trying to let my impatience release as I exhale.

"In a lot of sports and games, we focus on trying to beat our opponent," my mother says as we lift our hands to the sky again. "In yoga, there is no winning, no competition. You don't compare yourself to the person standing on the mat next to you because every body is different. On your exhale, fold forward."

We bend over, and I notice that Thermos can touch her toes, and Nick can tuck his hands under his feet. My hands don't even touch the ground.

"Just rest in this position for a moment," my mother says. "Notice how your body feels. Breathe in and breathe out. It doesn't matter how far you can bend. Your only goal is to become aware of your body and what it can do."

I breathe in and try to imagine doing yoga with Mr. Lamb. He makes everything a competition, even getting a drink at the fountain. I imagine Ryan Rakefield doing yoga. He'd definitely be comparing himself to everyone in the class, announcing that he was better than everyone. It's probably not in the spirit of yoga, but I imagine myself sneaking up behind Ryan when he's doing a forward fold and tipping him over. He'd do an accidental somersault and land sprawled on his back with no idea what had happened. I smile, suddenly feeling very calm and peaceful.

"Okay, everyone, now we are going to try tree pose. Standing straight, lift your left foot and place it on the inside of your right leg, either above or below your knee."

I watch Ari and her friends tuck their feet against their thighs, and it doesn't look too hard, so I copy them—and tip over to the right, knocking down Nick as I go.

"If it's hard to balance," my mother says as she stands effortlessly on one foot with her arms raised in a wide V, "put your heel on your ankle and let your toes rest on the ground."

I do as she says, but I am the only one who has to. Even Henry and Ruby are balancing fine. And even with my toes on the ground I still wobble. I'm not cut out for gym, any kind of gym. And I have to get ready to launch my campaign on Monday. I can't be wasting my time pretending to be a tree.

"Psst!" I hop myself closer to Thermos, then lift

up my foot again. "I thought of a theme for my campaign: Charlie Chaplin."

"Now, gently lower your left leg and switch sides." My mother demonstrates and everyone changes legs slowly and smoothly. Except me. I wobble onto my left foot, and lean over to Thermos.

"Any ideas?"

Thermos keeps looking straight ahead, but whispers, "Who's Charlie Chaplin again? A piano player?"

I nearly fall, but put my right foot on the ground to steady myself. "He's an old silent-movie star! You've definitely seen pictures of him, he's got a funny little mustache, a round black hat, and really baggy pants. And he walks funny and carries a cane."

Thermos nods like she's remembering, but she doesn't seem too sure. "Maybe you should choose someone a little more famous."

"He used to be the most famous person in the world." I throw my hands up in the air for emphasis, and fall backward. "You just don't realize that you know who he is."

My mother tells us to lunge forward with our left foot and extend one arm in front and one arm behind. "This is called warrior two. Try to feel yourself expanding out in all directions."

I get myself into position, and see Thermos watching me with a worried look. "I'm not going to fall. I've got both feet on the ground this time."

"Maybe you could pass out pictures of Charlie Chaplin."

"Maybe," I agree, wiggling myself back to the center of my mat. I can't believe Thermos doesn't know who Charlie is. He's hilarious. I lean over to Nick. "You know who Charlie Chaplin is, right?"

Nick switches his lunge from his left foot to his right, and almost knocks me in the head when he reverses the position of his arms. "Is he the guy with the funny mustache? I think you and I watched one of his movies last year. *The Little Kid*?"

"The Kid." I press my lips together, wondering if Ari and Thermos are right. My mother leads us through several more poses, all with strange names like downward facing dog and camel pose and

happy baby. I wobble my way through each of them, wondering the whole time if I should throw Charlie in the trash or stick with my gut.

At the end of the yoga lesson, my mother tells us to lie down on our mats with our eyes closed for deep relaxation. As I lie in the backyard with the sun on my face and a light breeze tickling the hairs on my arms, my mother talks in a quiet voice.

"Most of you probably didn't know much about yoga before we started today, so congratulations on having an open mind and trying something new. I hope you can take this attitude with you off the mat and be excited about learning new things in all your classes, and even during recess and after school. Now I'd like you to spend your final minutes of yoga focusing on your breath, noticing the cool air flowing in and the warm air flowing out."

I try to do as my mother says, but her words have gotten my brain going. Open mind. Learn new things. During recess.

"I've got it!" I bolt upright with my finger in the air.

"Louie!" My mother shakes her head at me. "We're supposed to be silent during deep relaxation."

Ari's got her hand on her chest. "You scared me to death." Her friends give me dirty looks.

"My heart is racing."

"That was, like, the opposite of relaxing."

I cringe, and look at Nick and Thermos. "Sorry, everyone."

Thermos leans over to us. "I almost wet my pants," she whispers.

"I did wet my pants!" Ruby stands up and points to a small puddle on her mat.

"Oh, Ruby." My mother grabs Ruby's hand and pulls her away from the mat. "Let's go inside and get you changed. Louie, I'm going to let you hose off Ruby's mat."

Gross.

Ari and her friends laugh as they walk away to sit in the tree fort, and Ruby waddles behind my mother into the house.

Henry hops back and forth on his mat as I grab the hose from the holder on the side of the garage.

"Uh, Henry," Nick says. "Do you need to use the bathroom, too?"

Henry doesn't even bother to answer. He just runs inside as fast as he can.

I turn on the hose and aim it at Ruby's mat. Once it's soaked I pick it up by the corner and hang it on our clothesline to dry. "Remind me never to use the purple mat if we have to do this again," I tell Nick and Thermos as I put away the hose.

Nick and Thermos look at me. "Well?" Nick finally says.

"Well what?"

"You just made us all jump out of our skin. Aren't you going to tell us why?"

"Oh yeah." I smile and nod. "I am going to open everyone's mind," I tell them. "Monday. At recess. I'll be giving lessons in Charlie Chaplin."

WALKING LESSONS

On Monday morning, Ryan Rakefield gets his campaign in full gear. His theme is vampires and his slogan is *I Vant to Valk in Your Parade.* Before school he passes out little vampire erasers and pencils that say *Vote for the Vampire.* At recess he passes out plastic vampire teeth. We are only supposed to distribute things we make ourselves, like campaign buttons, flyers, and stickers, but of course no one tells on him. Not even me. And since he's passing everything out before school and at recess, no teachers are around to notice.

During class, Violet hands out a list of Halloween safety tips, just like she promised. Mrs. Adler posts it on the bulletin board. Ryan gives everyone homemade stickers of his face with fangs. In my opinion, it's not all that different from his regular look. Mrs. Adler asks me if I have anything to pass out, but I tell her not yet. I will be offering my own special items. They just aren't things you can hold in your hands. Customized costume jokes and part one of my Charlie Chaplin—education series: Learn to Walk like the Tramp lessons.

By lunch recess, only one person has asked for a joke: Ava. Okay, well, she didn't exactly ask me, she asked Nick if I had made him a joke yet, but since I was standing right there, I told her a joke. Nick wasn't answering her anyway.

"What did the first pea in the pod say to the second pea in the pod? Peas to meet you."

One joke down, twenty to go.

No one has signed up for my walking lessons. Yet.

I rub my coupon and whisper a wish: "Help me get kids to sign up!" Then I press on my fake Charlie mustache and waddle around the playground.

Whenever I see anyone who looks like they are trying to figure out what to do next, I shuffle over, using a stick as my cane. "I'm walking like the most famous character of all time. Want me to teach you to do it, too? Lessons start by the chin-up bars in five minutes."

Here are some of the responses I've received so far:

"Are you Donald Duck?"

"Why are you walking like that? Do you have to go to the bathroom?"

"I think your shoes might be too tight. You should get them checked."

I'd probably have more success if I was wearing my entire Charlie Chaplin costume, but I think the costume will have a bigger impact if I save it until my speech.

After a few minutes of strolling the playground, I head over to the chin-up bars to meet Thermos and Nick. "Any luck?"

Thermos shakes her head. "Everyone I asked said they already know how to walk."

"How about you?" I ask Nick. "Hey! Wait a minute! What's that?" I point to the homemade button on his sweatshirt that says *Candy Rots Your Teeth. Vote for Violet.*

Nick shrugs. "She asked me to wear it. I'm not going to vote for her, but I didn't want to hurt her feelings."

I run both hands through my hair. "What am I going to do? This isn't working. If I could get one volunteer, I'm sure everyone would realize how much fun it is and then they'd join in."

"We-ll," Thermos says slowly. Then she points the top of her head at the swings a couple of times. Ava is there with three of her friends.

"I don't know." I search the playground for Ryan. "I should stay away from Ava. I don't need any teasing right now."

"Nick could ask her," Thermos says. "She'd say yes for sure!"

Nick tilts his head forward so his hair falls in his eyes. "Uh-uh," he says. "I can't."

"She might be Louie's only chance to get the lessons going."

"Please!" I clasp my hands together. "She's not that bad!"

Thermos laughs. "Uh, Louie. I don't think that's the problem."

I look at Nick. He's peeling some glue off his palm, leftover from art, acting like he didn't hear what Thermos said. "What do you mean?" I ask. "Nick, do you . . . do you *like* Ava?"

I can't believe I asked that. How could Nick *like* a girl? Liking a girl is worse than liking sports.

"No way!" Nick says. "I mean, I think she's nice."

I let out a sigh of relief. "Okay, then. Glad we agree." Thermos shakes her head at me like she doesn't believe it, but she doesn't say anything. Nick opens his mouth to say something, then shuts it.

I decide to risk it. "Okay. *I'll* go ask Ava to take walking lessons. Nick, you don't have to talk to her, but it's my only hope." Nick looks disappointed, but he'll get over it.

On my way to the swing set, I grab my coupon and give it a squeeze for good luck. It's starting to get real soft and wrinkly. I hope I don't wear it out.

"Hey, there, ladies and ladies." Ava, Hannah, and a couple of other girls stop swinging when I step in front of them. "This is your chance to learn to walk like one of the funniest comedians ever! Follow me!" I beckon to them.

"Is Nick going to do it?" Ava drags her feet on the ground until her swing stops.

"Barf course!" I say.

Ava climbs off her swing and turns her back to me so she can talk with her friends. Two of the girls shake their heads, but Hannah peers around Ava and looks at me with her nose half wrinkled. I swing my stick around like Charlie swung his cane.

Hannah rolls her eyes but says to Ava, "Oooh-kay."

They follow me back to the chin-up bars and stand next to Nick and Thermos.

"Okay, first everyone grab a cane." I start the lesson by pointing to the big pile of sticks I've collected. Everyone picks one up.

"Second, turn out your toes so that your feet make a big wide V."

I check to make sure that my students are doing it correctly, then I give them the last step. "Now keep your back nice and straight and pretend your feet hurt a lot. Charlie says the tramp always had sore feet. Okay, walk!"

The four of them start waddling around, and they look pretty good. "Hannah, make sure you keep your toes pointed out. Good."

I watch everyone for a minute more, then tell them to stop. "Okay, you've got the basic walk down, now we can add a couple of advanced techniques. First is the cane twirl. Sometimes as Charlie would walk down the street, he'd spin his cane like this."

I demonstrate by walking in a straight line while twirling my cane.

"Cool," says Grant, coming over to where we are standing. "What are you doing?"

"I'm giving lessons on how to walk like Charlie Chaplin. Want to try?"

"I don't know who Charlie Chaplin is, but why not?"

"Grab a cane," I tell him. "Nick and Thermos will fill you in. Okay, try the twirl!"

When everyone has gotten the twirl down pat, I teach them the knee hop and the skid: two of Chaplin's funniest moves. I can't believe how well it's going. I reach back into my pocket and rub my lucky coupon as a thank-you. As more kids on the playground notice what we are doing, they come over to watch and some even join in. Then Ava tries to do a left-footed skid and falls down on her side.

SHUFF

THUD

I hobble over and give her a hand up. "Don't worry. I probably fell a million times when I was first trying to teach myself how to walk like Charlie. You'll get the hang of it."

"Louie's holding hands with his girlfriend!"

I let go of Ava's hand so fast you'd think it was on fire. I didn't even know Ryan Rakefield was watching. I don't know how I let myself get so careless.

"Lesson's finished!" I waddle away from the group as fast as my Charlie Chaplin legs can shuffle and hide behind the rock wall. Hopefully, Ryan won't come after me. I hear footsteps and my heart starts pounding, but when I look up it's Nick and Thermos.

"Why'd you run away?" Thermos shakes her head like she can't believe it. "You had, like, eight kids there."

"Did he follow me? Is he still making fun of me? Were other people laughing?"

"Most kids stood around while Ryan made kissing noises," Thermos says. "They didn't understand why you ran away."

"This is terrible. Do you think everyone thinks Ava is my girlfriend?"

Thermos glances at Nick. His arms are folded across his chest.

"Not everyone," Thermos says.

o o o

After school, I go to my room and pin my coupon onto my bulletin board. I won't need it again until tomorrow and I want to keep it safe and sound. Then I head outside and find my dad and Ruby trying to string our ghosts up into the trees. The leaves are blazing red and mellow orange, but the ghosts are yellowy gray.

"Why don't ghosts need noses?" I ask.

"Because they can't smell their friends when they fly to the circus!" Ruby answers. "Get it?"

My dad and I look at each other and laugh. "Good one," I tell Ruby. She doesn't understand how to tell a joke, but she tries. I think the expression that fits here is: *A for effort.*

"Keep at it, Butterflyunicornjokergirl." Dad pats

Ruby's head. "Okay, Louie. Why don't ghosts need noses?"

"Because they don't have boo-gers!"

Ruby cracks up and my dad smiles. "Clever," he says. "I wish my ghost decorations were as good as your ghost jokes."

I look up in the trees and squint my eyes. Most of the sheets are drooping in a way that feels more sad than scary. "They don't look that bad."

"They look squished is what they look." Dad climbs down from the step stool and peers around our oak tree and down the block. Then he snaps upright and stands sideways so the tree is directly between him and the street. "Have you seen the Armbrusters' house?" he whispers.

I peer around the tree and squint at the Armbrusters' house, then I spin and put my back against the tree bark like I can't let anyone see me. "I can't get a good look from here," I whisper. "Why do we have to act like secret agents?"

My dad cups his hand over his mouth so I can't see his lips move when he talks. "I don't want Mr. Armbruster to notice that I've been scoping out his decorations. He's upping his game this year, trying to have the best-decorated house in the neighborhood. If he thinks I've got any better decorations up my sleeve, he'll buy even more stuff than he already has."

I look around our yard at the piles of broken bats, droopy ghosts, and crumpled witches. "*Do* you have better decorations up your sleeve?"

My dad taps the side of his head. "Not yet," he says, "but I've got ideas."

"Right." I nod.

"I just have to figure out how to afford them." Dad picks up a Styrofoam tombstone that has a big chunk broken out of it and sighs. "He's got twelve deluxe mummies. Twelve! He's wiring his front porch to a sound system so trick-or-treaters will hear spooky sounds when they get to the front door. And he's got five fog machines! I can't even afford more than two hours of fog-machine solution."

"Speaking of buying things, how expensive would it be if I wanted to buy a Charlie Chaplin movie for every kid in my class?"

Dad laughs so hard he throws his head back and pats his chest. "Louie, that's so far out of our budget we'd need a telescope to see it."

"What about buying canes for everyone, or fake mustaches?"

Dad shakes his head and ruffles my hair. "Still too expensive, I'm afraid. Though you're getting closer to our zip code." Dad passes me a box of black rubbery things. "Now help me hang these bats."

"Okay." I feel my heart sinking because I won't be able to compete with Ryan. I already gave my best effort—walking lessons—and he ruined it. I climb the step stool and tie a bat onto the lowest branch of our crab apple tree. "I don't think my classmates understand enough about Charlie Chaplin. I'll never win if they don't know who he is!"

My dad thinks about this for a second. "What

about changing your costume? Be something every-one understands, like a ghost or a mummy."

I pick another bat out of the box and stare at it. My dad doesn't get it. I need to be Charlie Chaplin, and I need to win as Charlie Chaplin.

"I know," Dad says. "You should be Dracula! A vampire is a great costume."

My hands tighten, and I accidentally pop the bat's head off. It flies through the air and hits the back of my dad's head as he is hanging our glow-in-the-dark skeleton. He stumbles forward and cracks the skeleton's rib cage against our oak tree.

"Louie! I don't want to spend my Halloween bud-get replacing broken decorations! How am I sup-posed to compete with deluxe mummies now?"

"Sorry," I say. "But you—"

"Go on inside with your sister." He looks the skeleton up and down. "I need to see if I can glue this together."

I want to argue with him, but at that moment I hear a squeak, and when I look up, I see Jamal riding his bike away from my house as fast as he can go. Great. He's probably going to tell Ryan about our broken decorations. About how even my dad thinks my Charlie Chaplin costume is doomed. And tomorrow Ryan will spend the entire day teasing me about it.

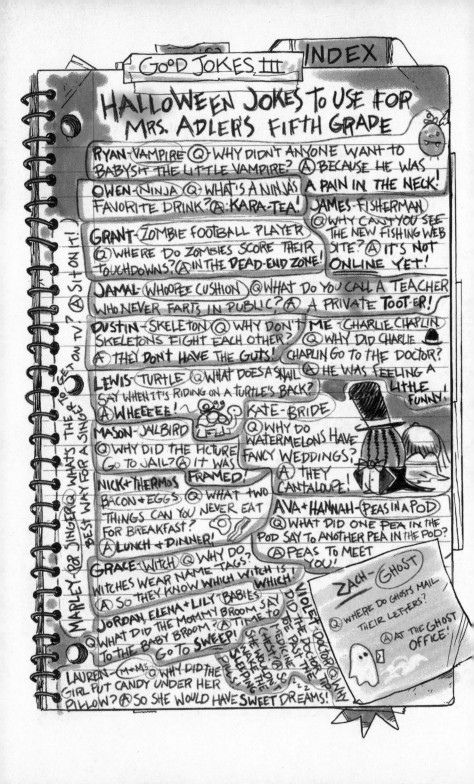

GOOD JOKES III

HALLOWEEN JOKES TO USE FOR MRS. ADLER'S FIFTH GRADE

RYAN - VAMPIRE Q: WHY DIDN'T ANYONE WANT TO BABYSIT THE LITTLE VAMPIRE? A: BECAUSE HE WAS A PAIN IN THE NECK!

OWEN - NINJA Q: WHAT'S A NINJA'S FAVORITE DRINK? A: KARA-TEA!

JAMES - FISHERMAN Q: WHY CAN'T YOU SEE THE NEW FISHING WEB SITE? A: IT'S NOT ONLINE YET!

GRANT - ZOMBIE FOOTBALL PLAYER Q: WHERE DO ZOMBIES SCORE THEIR TOUCHDOWNS? A: IN THE DEAD-END ZONE!

JAMAL - WHOOPEE CUSHION Q: WHAT DO YOU CALL A TEACHER WHO NEVER FARTS IN PUBLIC? A: A PRIVATE TOOT-ER!

DUSTIN - SKELETON Q: WHY DON'T SKELETONS FIGHT EACH OTHER? A: THEY DON'T HAVE THE GUTS!

ME - CHARLIE CHAPLIN Q: WHY DID CHARLIE CHAPLIN GO TO THE DOCTOR? A: HE WAS FEELING A LITTLE FUNNY!

LEWIS - TURTLE Q: WHAT DOES A SNAIL SAY WHEN IT'S RIDING ON A TURTLE'S BACK? A: WHEEEEE!

KATE - BRIDE Q: WHY DO WATERMELONS HAVE FANCY WEDDINGS? A: THEY CANTALOUPE!

MASON - JAILBIRD Q: WHY DID THE PICTURE GO TO JAIL? A: IT WAS FRAMED!

NICK + THERMOS BACON + EGGS Q: WHAT TWO THINGS CAN YOU NEVER EAT FOR BREAKFAST? A: LUNCH + DINNER!

AVA + HANNAH - PEAS IN A POD Q: WHAT DID ONE PEA IN THE POD SAY TO ANOTHER PEA IN THE POD? A: PEAS TO MEET YOU!

GRACE - WITCH Q: WHY DO WITCHES WEAR NAME TAGS? A: SO THEY KNOW WHICH WITCH IS WHICH!

JORDAN, ELENA + LILY - BABIES Q: WHAT DID THE MOMMY BROOM SAY TO THE BABY BROOM? A: TIME TO GO TO SWEEP!

VIOLET - DOCTOR Q: WHY DID THE DOCTOR TIP-TOE PAST THE MEDICINE CHEST? SO SHE WOULDN'T WAKE THE SLEEPING PILLS!

ZACH - GHOST Q: WHERE DO GHOSTS MAIL THEIR LETTERS? A: AT THE GHOST OFFICE!

LAUREN - M+M's Q: WHY DID THE GIRL PUT CANDY UNDER HER PILLOW? A: SO SHE WOULD HAVE SWEET DREAMS!

MARLEY - POP SINGER Q: WHAT'S THE BEST WAY FOR A SINGER TO GET ON TV? A: SIT ON IT!

NEVER MAKE A BIG P

When I get to school on Tuesday, I hide behind the rock wall until the bell rings. I don't want to give Ryan any chances to tease me. During the Pledge of Allegiance, I take a quick count of campaign buttons to see how the election is looking. Most of the girls are wearing Violet's anti-candy buttons and most of the boys are wearing Ryan's *Vote for the Vampire* buttons. Only three people are wearing the *Vote for Louie. He's a Classic!* buttons I made last night: Nick, Thermos, and me.

I'm starting to wonder if it's possible to win this election. There must be something I can do, but I don't know what it is yet. I do know one thing though. Being teased is not going to help my campaign. I don't raise my hand once the entire morning. You never know when you are going to say something that you could be teased for. For example, you might mess up when you write the heading *Plants* at the top of your science lab sheet. Then you will say, "Mrs. Adler, could I have a new sheet, my *p* is too big." Then Ryan will start telling everyone you made a big *pee* on your paper. And everyone will laugh and say you were trying to fertilize your plants.

That didn't actually happen. *Really.*

When it comes to teasing, you can never be too careful. The best way to avoid teasing is to remove yourself from the situation. During lunch, I hide in the bathroom. During lunch recess, I squat behind a clump of bushes even though Nick and Thermos offer to play Don't Make Me Laugh: Swing-Set Edition. I'm tempted, but the swing set is too close to the basketball court and Ryan Rakefield is definitely capable of dribbling and teasing at the same time. When we go inside, my stomach twists. In five minutes, Mrs. Adler is going to tell our class to line up for gym. If I have to dance with Ava in front of Ryan, I know he's going to make smooch sounds. It'll be the kiss of death. I've got to think of something. Fast.

"Okay, class, everyone to the door!"

In the commotion of chairs scraping back and bodies shuffling around me to get a spot in line, I grab a pair of scissors from my desk and casually reach down while looking around the room to make sure no one notices what I'm doing. Then I snip a bunch of notches in my laces, throw the scissors back in my desk, and line up.

"What took you so long?" Nick asks as I step up behind him.

I shrug innocently, but my heart thumps.

When we get to gym and Mr. Lamb tells us to step into our squares with our partners, I exclaim loudly, "Oh no! My shoes are untied."

I bend down to tie them and make sure I pull the laces as hard as I can. At first they don't break like I'm expecting them to, but I tug a little more and—*snap*. "Oh no!" I shout again. "My laces broke! I guess I have to sit out."

I stand and walk to the bleachers, but Mr. Lamb clomps over to me in his cowboy boots and puts a hand on my shoulder. He looks me up and down. "It's been quite a while since you participated in gym."

I make a sad face and nod. "I know. I have bad luck, I guess."

I start off toward the bleachers again, but Mr. Lamb says, "Try dancing in your socks."

There is no way, *no way*, I am going to square dance with Ava *in my socks*. That's practically like dancing *naked*! There is only one way out and even though I know it's going to be painful, I've got no other choice. I take off my shoes, take a step toward Ava, and let myself do a major banana-peel slip. I land flat on my back. A bunch of kids snicker, and Ryan calls out, "Put your shoes on, I can smell your feet from here!" But Mr. Lamb frowns at me and points at the bleachers, so I don't care.

After I'm settled in my seat Mr. Lamb tells my class that today we are going to get a chance to put all the moves that we've learned so far into practice. "I will turn on the music, then call out the steps. You follow along to what the caller— that's me—announces. This is how our assessment will work as well, but we'll use more steps. Where are my demonstrators? Jamal? Lauren?"

Jamal and Lauren walk to the front of the gym. Well, Lauren walks and Jamal sort of drags his feet. I don't know what he's so worried about since he's the best dancer in our whole class. Probably in our whole grade.

Mr. Lamb turns on the music and starts calling out steps, but whatever step he calls, Jamal does something different. Whichever direction he's supposed to go, he goes the wrong way. He even trips and falls during the do-si-do. Mr. Lamb throws his hands in the air and shuts off the music halfway through the demonstration. "I don't know what's gotten into you today. Hopefully the rest of

you will do a little better than that. Take your places!"

Jamal races back to his square, and when the whole class starts dancing to Mr. Lamb's calls, I notice that Jamal is now able to follow the directions without a problem. It's very strange.

Ava has to dance by herself. She looks over at me a bunch of times, and I stare down through the gap in the bleachers like I'm looking for something that fell to the ground, because I feel a little guilty about making her dance by herself.

When the class is finished and we line up, Jamal says, "I must be the worst dancer ever. I'm so bad my shoes were trying to run away from me while I danced."

"Yeah," Ryan Rakefield agrees. "You were so bad, you made Mr. Lamb cry."

They both laugh at that, while I keep myself quiet at the back of the line. I don't get it. Jamal is helping Ryan to tease him.

"I hope you won't have to miss gym next time, Louie." Ava loses her place in line to stand next to me.

I scratch my elbow and say, "Hmmm," so that I'm not ignoring her, but no one will notice us talking either. It seems to be working. The only person looking at us is Nick, five people ahead of us. He squints his eyes and frowns.

ALL BURGERS
ON DECK

After dinner, Dad covers the kitchen table with newspaper, then puts out five pumpkins. It's the Burger Annual Pumpkin-Carving Night. Another one of our Halloween traditions. My father hands each of us a black marker for planning our design, and a special bumpy pumpkin-cutting knife. Then he stands at the head of the table and claps his hands once. "Burgers! It's time for us to get serious about Halloween! The Armbrusters have put spooky faces on their trees and have purchased jumbo inflatables for the corners of their lawn. But pumpkin carving is the category where we can really shine. No simple smiling jack-o'-lanterns this year! We've got to bring it, Burgers, or the famous Burger Halloween Reputation is going to become a faint chocolate-scented memory."

"I'm carving mine into a unipumkorn!" says Ruby. "I've already imagined how to do it."

"That's the spirit!" My dad gives her a high five.

"Well, I think it's a nice compliment," my mother says. "The Armbrusters were always such big fans of your decorating. Remember how you gave Roger that guided tour of our yard last year? Imitation is the sincerest form of flattery, you know."

"That may be true, but it's also a challenge. This is Decoration War, and we are at a disadvantage. All Burgers have to pull their weight."

"Aye, aye, Captain!" Ruby says, saluting my dad.

"I helped hang up the bats," I remind him.

"I'm telling you"—Ari stretches a long string of gum out of her mouth and then drops it back in— "four words. Full. Size. Candy. Bars."

"We are not going to rot children's mouths out, and this isn't a war." My mother laughs. She starts sketching on her pumpkin. "Halloween is a time when the community gets together to give kids a fun neighborhood adventure. The more houses that decorate with gusto the better. But I do love to carve a pumpkin! I'm going to make one of those fancy picture pumpkins this year." My mother turns her pumpkin around so we can see the beginnings of her drawing. "It's a basketball! A glowing basketball for Halloween. Oooh, maybe I'll make one for school, too."

"A winner!" My dad gives her two thumbs up. Then he gets to work sketching his own pumpkin.

"I still think we need good candy. No one goes to a house because they heard the pumpkins were great." Ari chews on the cap of her marker and studies her blank pumpkin.

"It's not just one thing that makes a house fun." My dad winks at my mom. "It's the total of everything we do. Great pumpkins, healthy snacks, spooky decorations. I know we can think of ways to make our house the best."

"Of course we can," my mother agrees. "We're the Burgers! What if we offer free high fives to every trick-or-treater?"

"Yeah!" Ruby grabs her safety knife and starts sawing along the lines she drew. "Also, we should have a real unicorn and we can give everyone unicorn rides and we can pass out baby unicorns."

"That would be pretty spectacular," my mother says.

"Well, if you're not doing full-size candy," Ari says, "then you should at least make our house super scary. Like, maybe an axe murderer could jump out of the bushes and grab each person walking

up the sidewalk." Ari uncaps her marker and starts drawing with one eye closed.

I start my sketch, too. I'm going to carve the symbol for pi, π. Pumpkin pie.

"Hmmm," my mother says to Ari. "Maybe we can start that once it gets dark. I don't want to frighten the little kids. But a lot of my students said they'd come by. I'd like to give them a good scare! Show them gym teachers know how to have fun."

"I don't know," I say. "These are good ideas, but the Armbrusters will still have more stuff than us. It's hard to compete with someone who can buy things when you can't." I think of Ryan and his glow sticks and vampire teeth.

My dad doesn't say anything. He bites his bottom lip and draws a few more lines on his pumpkin. Then he turns it around so we can see his design: five hamburgers. "The Burgers!" he says.

"I love it!" My mother rubs my back. "The Armbrusters might have more stuff than us, Louie, and they might even get more trick-or-treaters than us, but that doesn't mean we can't enjoy our Halloween."

"Of course not!" My father flourishes his carving knife and jabs it into the top of his pumpkin. He takes a deep breath. "It's a matter of adjusting our expectations."

Maybe that works for trick-or-treating, but I don't want to adjust my expectations. I want to win class marshal. When we finish carving our pumpkins, and everyone heads off in their separate directions, I follow Ari to her room.

"What?" she says when she realizes I am behind her.

"I've got to ask you a question. About being popular."

"Hold on." Ari sends a text and then invites me to sit on her shaggy pink carpet. She sits on her bed. "Go for it."

"Well, hypothetically speaking, if a person wanted to win a popularity contest, and they weren't already popular, how could they make a bump happen?"

Ari chews on her thumb, thinking. "Here's the thing about bumps. You can't create them or make them happen. *They just happen.* That's why they work. If you could create a bump then everyone would be popular, but everyone can't be popular, because you can't have popular unless you have unpopular, too."

"But—but then how do I—I mean, how could someone win a popularity contest?"

She shrugs. "Maybe they can't. Some people weren't meant to be popular. It's not the end of the world."

I crawl over to the doorway. That wasn't the answer I wanted to hear.

"Or . . ." Ari holds her finger up like she's got a great idea. I turn around hopefully. "You might get lucky and be attacked by zombies. That should give you at least three days of popularity."

BARFTASTIC WAYS TO AVOID GYM

SHODDY SHOELACES: FIRST, CUT A NOTCH ON EITHER SIDE OF BOTH SHOELACES. SECOND, GO TO GYM WITH YOUR SHOELACES UNTIED. THIRD, ANNOUNCE LOUDLY THAT YOU ARE GOING TO TIE YOUR LACES. FOURTH, PULL UNTIL THE LACES SNAP. OOPS! CAN'T PLAY DODGEBALL IF YOU DON'T HAVE LACES!

IT'S NOT EASY BEING GREEN: FIRST, GO TO THE BATHROOM WITH A GREEN MARKER AND COLOR ALL OVER YOUR FACE. SECOND, WASH THE MARKER OFF YOUR FACE LEAVING ONLY A SLIGHT GREEN TINGE BEHIND. THIRD, GO TO GYM WITH YOUR ARMS WRAPPED AROUND YOUR STOMACH AND YOUR MOUTH IN A SAD FROWN. FOURTH, WHEN YOUR GYM TEACHER SAYS IT'S TIME TO PICK TEAMS, DOUBLE OVER AND SHOUT, "I THINK I ATE SOMETHING FUNNY!" TOO BAD! CAN'T PLAY FLAG FOOTBALL WHEN YOU'RE SICK!

HUMAN DOMINOES: FIRST, WALK TO GYM IN LINE WITH THE REST OF YOUR CLASS. SECOND, BEFORE YOUR CLASS GETS OUT OF LINE (OR IF THEY GET IN LINE FOR SOMETHING ELSE), FALL OVER AND KNOCK DOWN THE PERSON NEXT TO YOU, SO THAT THEY KNOCK DOWN THE PERSON NEXT TO THEM, AND THE NEXT PERSON KNOCKS DOWN THE PERSON NEXT TO THEM AND SO ON, AND SO ON. DARN! CAN'T RUN THE PACER IF EVERYONE HAS TO GO TO THE NURSE'S OFFICE.

BURGER WITH A SIDE OF BLOODY NOSE: FIRST, GRAB A KETCHUP PACKET NEXT TIME YOU ARE IN THE CAFETERIA. SECOND, BRING THE KETCHUP PACKET TO GYM. THIRD, WHEN NO ONE IS LOOKING, SQUEEZE THE KETCHUP ONTO YOUR FACE RIGHT UNDER YOUR FAVORITE NOSTRIL. FOURTH, JUST WAIT. SOMEONE WILL DEFINITELY TELL YOUR GYM TEACHER YOU HAVE A BLOODY NOSE. RATS! CAN'T DO JUMPING JACKS WITH A GUSHING SMELLER.

CAUGHT RED-HANDED: FIRST, COVER YOUR HANDS WITH RED MARKER AND A LITTLE BIT OF GLUE. SECOND, WALK TO GYM WITH YOUR HANDS IN YOUR POCKETS SO NOBODY SEES THEM. THIRD, WHEN YOUR GYM TEACHER BRINGS OUT THE BALLS, HOLD UP YOUR HANDS AND SAY YOU FORGOT TO WASH THEM BEFORE GYM. FOURTH, SCRUB YOUR HANDS IN THE BATHROOM UNTIL YOU GET EVERY SPECK OF SKIN CLEAN. UH-OH! IT TAKES A **REALLY** LONG TIME TO GET THAT MUCH MARKER OFF. IT MIGHT EVEN TAKE ALL OF GYM. NO GYM!

I'LL BE A MONKEY'S ANKLE: FIRST, GO TO GYM ACTING LIKE YOU CAN'T WAIT TO PARTICIPATE. SECOND, RAISE YOUR HAND HIGHER THAN ANYONE ELSE WHEN YOUR GYM TEACHER ASKS WHO WANTS TO DEMONSTRATE. THIRD, WHEN YOUR GYM TEACHER CALLS ON YOU, DEMONSTRATE WITH LOTS OF ENTHUSIASM. SO MUCH ENTHUSIASM THAT IT KNOCKS YOU OVER. FOURTH, WHEN YOU GET UP, DON'T PUT ANY PRESSURE ON YOUR LEAST FAVORITE FOOT. WHEN YOUR GYM TEACHER SEES YOU LIMPING HE WILL MAKE YOU SIT ON THE SIDELINES. BUMMER! YOU REALLY WANTED TO PARTICIPATE TODAY.

PERMANENT B.U.R.P.

By Wednesday, I feel the election slipping
away from me. I can't keep up with wax vampire
lips, fake blood, and Dracula tattoos. I need something as powerful as full-size candy bars. So I'm
going to try something risky: bringing my comedy
notebook to school. Comedy gave me my very first
bump. If my stand-up routine got me a bump,
maybe my notebook can give me another bump.
One big enough to win an election. I plan to read
bits of the notebook at recess and at lunchtime.
I could also give people tips on how to keep their
own notebooks and write their own catchphrases.
This could be barfmongous!

I'm about to leave for school when I realize I

forgot my coupon. If I'm bringing my notebook, I'm going to need good luck. I race down the hall to my bedroom, but the coupon is not on my bulletin board anymore. The little black pushpin is holding up air. I search the floor, under my bed, in my clothes hamper. I can't find it anywhere.

Finally my dad calls, "Louie! Nick, Henry, and Ruby are waiting for you!"

I give up my search and slump outside to the sidewalk.

When I get to school, Nick suggests we play Antidisestablishmentarianism with Thermos, but I say no. I toss my backpack on the ground and run over to Grant by the tetherball pole. I ask him if he wants to hear something funny, and then read him my entry about choosing a Halloween costume. By the time I'm halfway through, Owen and Hannah are listening, too. They even laugh a little. After I've finished, I look around for someone else to read to, but Ryan blocks my path. "What's that? Diary of a Wimpy Burger?" He tries to grab my notebook out of my hands. I snatch it away. I thought he was playing basketball. Dustin and James try to help Ryan get my notebook, and they chase me around the playground until the bell rings.

The morning only gets worse. Mrs. Adler makes us watch a video about electric circuits in science and I fall asleep. I dream that I am driving a vacuum tractor around the school. In front of me there is a big puddle, so I shout, "Water and electricity don't mix!" Then I wake up and see that there is a big puddle of drool on my desk.

That didn't actually happen. *Really.*

Mrs. Adler holds a spelling bee and I get out first, on the word *ewe*. I spelled it y-o-u. I believe the expression I should have used is: *May I have the definition, please.*

I'm not feeling hopeful when it's time to go out for recess, but when I reach inside my desk to grab my comedy notebook I feel hope*less*. It's gone! Nick and Thermos help me look under my desk and in my locker until Mrs. Adler tells us we have to go outside. We spend our entire recess asking every single person in fifth grade if they've seen it, but no one says yes. I feel even lower than a B.U.R.P. I feel like a C.L.A.M.: Complete Loser And Moron. I never should have brought my notebook to school. I never should have let my coupon leave my sight. This terrible day would not have happened if I still had it.

Finally, when the world's most disastrous day is over, I grab my bag and walk to Nick's locker. Ryan blocks my way. "Drool boy, why don't you just drop out of the race and save yourself the misery."

I want to climb into my backpack and zip myself inside. I try to walk around him, but he steps to the side and blocks my way again. He leans forward and whispers in my ear: "No one will vote for a B.U.R.P."

My hands go icy and my ears catch fire. Ryan knows my secret acronym.

I swallow hard and reach for my coupon, but then I remember that it's gone.

Ryan has my notebook. I can't think of anything worse. I want to tell him to give it back, but my voice is stuck.

"I'll never be your chauffeur. You'll be *my* assistant. It doesn't matter if you were on TV. Everyone always votes for me. I'm the tallest kid in the class." Ryan turns away from me so that the rest of the kids in the hall will hear what he says next. "If you vote for me, my mom will pass out hot chocolate at my house after school on Halloween. With whipped cream *and* marshmallows."

"I'd like to point out that given the amount of candy we get on Halloween, the last thing we need is a sugary beverage." Violet steps in front of Ryan. "Think about a healthy Halloween! If you vote for me, then my parents will pass out toothbrushes and sugar-free gum after school. You can thank me the next time you visit the dentist."

Everyone turns and looks at me, as if they are waiting to see what I will offer. But I am in a fog. My knees shake. The only thing I can think about is my notebook, and how, in Ryan's hands, it could become the ultimate weapon of Louie destruction.

"You guys!" Thermos says. "Those things happen after the parade. Think about during the parade. Won't it be fun if we all walk like Charlie Chaplin?"

"But what about after school?" Hannah asks. "What do we get if we vote for Louie?"

Thermos grabs my arm and nudges me forward.

I look at my classmates, but I've got nothing. What am I supposed to say? *If you vote for me, all you get is me?* That will never work.

"If you vote for me . . . uh." Sweat beads form on my forehead. My legs quiver. "If you vote for me . . ." My mind is a blank.

"If you vote for me, *I'll* tell you jokes," Ryan says. "Hey, Owen. What's a ninja's favorite drink? Kara-tea!"

Ryan does a karate chop as he delivers my punch line. It feels like the chop lands right in my gut. I reach into my back pocket again. All I feel is lint and a wood chip that must have gotten in there when I accidentally walked in front of the swings and got knocked over.

"If you vote for me . . ." Everyone is staring. I say the first thing that pops into my mind. "Zombies will attack me."

"What?" Owen says.

My classmates look at me like I'm insane. I think they might be right.

"Uh, zombies will attack my house." I have no idea what I'm going to say next, but I have to keep talking. "They will make a haunted zombie maze."

"Cool!" Grant says.

"And axe murderers will jump out of the bushes and grab you," I add.

"Awesome!" someone else says.

"Right," says Ryan. "Knowing you, it will be a little-kid maze, with nothing scary in it at all."

My eyes fly around the hallway. I'm desperately trying to think of something to convince people that whatever is happening at my house will be better than hot chocolate and toothbrushes. "It'll be crazy scary."

"What will it have?" asks Mason. "Will we wear blindfolds? Will zombies grab us and put ice down our backs? Will we reach into bowls to feel their eyeballs and intestines?"

"Sure," I say. "Whatever you want!"

"Unicorntastic," says a squeaky voice I don't recognize from my class. I look down and there is Ruby looking up at me. "We were worrying about where you were. But don't worry anymore. We found you. Can I feel the eyeballs?"

"Who cares about Halloween right now anyway," Ryan says. "I'm going to miss my bus."

As soon as he leaves, pretty much everyone else in my class leaves, too. Thermos whispers

something to Nick before she takes off for the bus line. Nick scowls at me.

What did *I* do?

"I want to wear a blindfold with ice cubes," Ruby says. "Can I come?"

"You're already invited, silly," says Henry. "It's Nick's birthday party."

"Oh," I say. *Oh.* So that's why Nick was upset. "I'm sorry. That was really stupid. My brain melts when I get too close to Ryan. It's like you when you have to talk with Ava."

Nick fiddles with the zipper on his backpack. "It's not the same thing."

"I know. Ava's nowhere near as bad as Ryan. Ryan Rakefield makes me do crazy things. He stole my comedy notebook." I lace my fingers together and hold my hands in front of my chest. "I plead temporary insanity. I'm not going to have a Halloween party."

"Really?"

"Yeah, my dad probably won't let me."

"That's the only reason why you aren't going to have a party? Ever since you decided to run for marshal you've become a different person."

I keep making this worse and worse. "No! I wouldn't have one even if he did let me. Not unless you said it was okay. And I wouldn't do any of the same things you're doing at your birthday party. I'd let you pick the coolest activities and I'd do the runner-up ones that you didn't have time for." I reach back and touch my wood chip. It doesn't seem to work like the coupon.

"Promise?" Nick asks.

"I barf swear," I say, and pretend to stick my finger down my throat.

"Okay," Nick says, though he acts like he doesn't quite trust me. "And you'll help me with my party?"

"I'm your best friend! Of course I'll help."

o o o

"Dad!" I shout when Ruby and I get home.

"Daddy!" Ruby throws her backpack down the hallway, kicks off her shoes, and lets them land wherever they want. "We're looking for you."

I put Ruby's things away nice and neat, then we both go searching for my dad. Just when I'm pretty sure he's not in the house, we hear a *crash* from the garage.

"I know where he is!" Ruby shouts.

In the garage, my dad is surrounded by bags of brand-new spiderweb fluff, zip-line ghosts, and animatronic black cats. There is a big cardboard box turned upside down next to the piles of stuff and my dad hurriedly flips it over and starts shoving the Halloween supplies inside.

"Oh, hi, guys. Did school end early today?"

"Nope." Ruby pets one of the cats, and it arches

its back and hisses. Ruby jumps. "Is that for the zombie maze?"

"Ruby," I say through clenched teeth. I need to ask my dad in my own way. Ruby can't go blurting everything out.

"Nothing is for anything yet," my dad says. "These are ideas. I'm not keeping everything, but I couldn't decide until I tried them out at our house."

I look at the giant box next to my dad. "That's a lot of stuff," I say.

Ruby nuzzles a fuzzy ghost. "I bet it costed a million zillion dollars."

"Not that much." My dad half laughs. "But we don't need to tell your mom because I got a discount, and I'm going to return a bunch of it anyway, so in the end I'll be right on budget. Or pretty close. Let's wait until I finish decorating so she can have a fun surprise."

I feel a funny little tickle in my throat. I cough. "A discount?"

My dad wipes his hand over his mouth. "Yes, about that. I had to borrow your coupon. Don't worry. I will still let you pick anything you want from the store, but it made sense to use it when I was making such a big purchase."

My eyes start to burn and I feel a sour lemon lodge itself at the base of my throat. My dad stole my coupon. He basically ruined my life.

"You used it already? It's gone?" I blink away some of the burn, but then suddenly it's as if my entire body is on fire. "You stole my coupon!" I shout.

"There is no need to get upset." My dad tries to calm me down, but I won't listen. I don't care if I can buy anything at the store. Because of him my day was a disaster. Who knows what would have happened if I had still had good luck. Maybe Ryan would have gotten five thousand paper cuts when he tried to steal my notebook and I'd have caught him red-handed. And then, maybe my comedy notebook plan would have worked, and I'd be known as a L.A.F.F.: Ludicrously Amusing and Funny Friend. All I know is I didn't get a bump, and it's my dad's fault.

"They don't sell the stuff I want at the store!" I feel a volcano erupting inside my body. I stamp my feet and I know I must look like a toddler having a temper tantrum, but I can't stop myself. "I want my coupon back!"

My dad blinks at me a bunch of times, but he doesn't say anything.

Ruby slides herself underneath my dad's work-table and tugs on my dad's pant leg. I forgot she was even in the garage. "Louie invited the whole fifth grade to our house for a zombie maze that will have the same things of Nick's birthday," she whispers.

"Forget it," I say. "I don't want it anymore." Even if my dad made a zombie maze, Ryan would figure out some way to ruin it.

My dad is still staring at me, rubbing his hands over his face. I need to get out of the garage. I take about ten steps toward the house, then my dad calls out, "Wait!"

I turn around.

"I'm sorry, Louie. I didn't realize it would be such a big deal."

I sigh. My dad does look sorry, but that doesn't change the facts. The last little bit of my fame and fortune is gone. And I know what that means: I'm going back to being a B.U.R.P.

GET OUT OF GYM FREE

As my class walks down death row (my new nickname for the hallway that leads to gym), it feels like the air is made of water. I can't breathe and my arms and legs move in slow motion. Who knows what Ryan has in store for me today if I can't fake my way out of class? I slide my hand into my pocket for the ketchup packet I snuck out of the cafeteria. After we line up next to our partners, I rip the edge of the packet and raise it to my nose, ready to fake a big gooey nosebleed. But the second before I squeeze, Jamal shouts, "My nose is bleeding."

Mr. Lamb grabs a tissue and shoves it at Jamal. "Go to the nurse's office," he barks.

I flinch, even though he wasn't barking at me.

Jamal holds the tissue to his nose with one hand. As he walks out the door, he puts his other hand in his pocket. I notice it is holding something small and white.

I quickly move my hand away from my nose and pretend I was straightening my hair. I have to figure out some way to get rid of my ketchup packet. I can't fake a bloody nose now. Mr. Lamb would be too suspicious.

"Oh my goodness," Ava shouts, gripping my shoulder. "Mr. Lamb! Louie's got a bloody ear!"

What?!

I run my fingers over my ear and they come away covered in ketchup. I must have squeezed my packet accidentally. Mr. Lamb storms over to me, frowning, and I tuck the empty packet in the waistband of my pants.

Mr. Lamb towers above me and I think he's going to yell, but he folds his arms across his chest, shakes his head, and points toward the door.

I slink out of the classroom, feeling kind of bad, though I don't know why. After all, I did get out of gym and that was the most important thing.

I'm halfway to the nurse's office when I see Jamal at the drinking fountain. A ketchup packet is sticking halfway out of his pocket.

"You!" I say, pointing at it. "You read my note-book."

Jamal stands up and shoves the ketchup back into his pocket. His eyes twitch nervously as he

looks up and down the hallway. "Uh, no I didn't. I don't know what you're talking about!"

"You did! I saw the ketchup." Jamal's hand moves toward his hip, but he stops it. He squeaks his shoe on the hallway floor. "I don't get it. Why do you care about missing gym? You're really good at square-dancing."

Jamal gets right in my face. I can smell the Cheetos he had for lunch. "I am *not*, and if you say so again, I'll tell everyone about your embarrassing moments and your weird words and all your other kooky thoughts!"

I back away from Jamal, hands in the air. He's read my entire notebook. "I won't say anything, I promise!"

Jamal nods at me, and then we just stand there in the hallway next to Barney the Barker Badger with nothing more to say.

"Uh, I'm going to use the boys' room and wash my ear before I go to the nurse."

"Yeah," Jamal says. "Me, too. I should wash my nose."

After we wash, we walk to the nurse. She gives both of us passes back to gym since there is nothing wrong with us. Mr. Lamb tells us to sit on the bleachers for the last five minutes of class, but when Mrs. Adler arrives, he tells me to stay put and I watch my whole class line up and leave while Mr. Lamb corners me on the bottom bleacher. He puts one foot on the step next to where I'm sitting and leans in to talk to me.

"I'm afraid your participation in gym hasn't improved, Mr. Burger."

I gulp. "Uh. I'm sorry?"

"Sorry doesn't help. You are flunking the square-dance unit, which means you are flunking gym this quarter."

I try to look serious, even though it doesn't seem like that big a deal. Flunking gym? Big whoop. I bet nothing even happens to you if you flunk gym.

"You know, if you are flunking a class, you can't participate in any extracurricular activities."

I keep a straight face, but inside I'm doing a happy dance. I don't even do extracurriculars! No basketball club for me? Darn. No student council meetings? I didn't even get elected for them.

"The next time we have gym, I want to see your feet moving. No excuses."

"Okay!" I nod solemnly, wondering if there is some way to get out of gym and keep my feet moving at the same time. Maybe I could wear malfunctioning wheelie shoes.

Mr. Lamb studies me and then tells me to go back to class. I walk slowly until I turn the corner from the gym. Then I click my heels and whisper, "Yes!" I can miss gym forever with no consequences.

o o o

On the way home from school, I brainstorm ways to get my notebook back. Nick and I could sneak out of our houses dressed like burglars and break into Ryan's bedroom. We could build a robot bodyguard to hold Ryan up by his feet until he tells us where it is. We could train a squirrel to follow Ryan home, jump in his backpack, and retrieve the notebook. I try to get Nick to help me come up with ideas, but he says he can't think of anything.

It's a little bit fun to think up the ways, but it's mostly depressing because I know none of them will work. And because Nick isn't helping. And because I have no idea what Ryan has in store for me. I wonder if it's safe to start a new notebook. I thought of a barfmazing entry: *How to booby-trap your sister's bedroom*, but I don't know if I want to write it down. My words used to make me feel better, but now I know they can be used against me. I say goodbye to Nick, then notice that my mother's car is parked in the driveway. She's home from work early, but I don't think anything of it until I walk into the garage.

My father is standing at his worktable with even more new Halloween supplies spread out around him and my mother is standing across from him rubbing her forehead.

My feet freeze in the doorway. My dad looks sheepish and small. Suddenly, I feel bad for him. He wasn't trying to do anything horrible. He wanted

our house to look great. It's not a crime. My mom picks up a set of mummy arms and sighs. She probably doesn't even realize that my dad was maybe not even going to keep all the decorations.

I tiptoe backward away from the garage. I don't want to watch whatever comes next.

"Hold on, Louie." My mother sets the mummy arms down and turns around.

"Me?" I hold my breath.

"Yes, you." My mother strides over to me, takes me by the shoulders, and steers me into one of the folding chairs in front of my stage. "We need to have a serious talk."

"I didn't know Dad was going to buy so much stuff. I didn't give him the coupon!"

My mother holds up one hand. "This is not about Halloween. Although we need to talk about that, too, because I never would have known about this unless I came home early." She presses her lips together and shakes her head. "But the reason I came home early today, Louie, is that I got a phone call from Mr. Lamb." She runs both hands through her hair. "Flunking gym, Louie? The gym teacher's kid? Flunking?"

"Louie!" My dad frowns at me, and steps out from behind his table to stand by my mother. "This is unacceptable."

"It's not as bad as you think, you guys." My palms start sweating, so I rub them on my pants. "The only consequence of flunking gym is I can't participate in extracurriculars, and I don't do extracurriculars! So that means there are no consequences."

"Louie, that's not the poi—" my dad starts to say, but my mom cuts him off.

"There are plenty of consequences to flunking gym. I don't even know how I'm going to face Mr. Lamb at the next phys ed committee meeting. The first thing you have to do is write him a letter of apology."

"Wha—" I start to say, but then I see the look on my mom's face and I say, "Okay."

"Next, you will make up what you've missed. My friend Carole Binkie owns a dance studio and one of her teachers has offered to give you *free* square-dance lessons so you can catch up to your class."

"But, Mom!" *Dance lessons?* This can't be happening!

"Finally, you will not miss any more gym classes. Gym is important on its own, but if that's not a good enough reason, then you should know that being in the Halloween parade is an extracurricular activity."

No Halloween parade? A cold trickle slides down my neck. I did not realize gym was this serious.

"Do I have your agreement?" My mother lowers her voice and takes my hand. "I know sometimes you don't believe you have athletic talent, Louie, but moving is important. You have to figure out your own way. And if not that, do it for me. Please."

I hang my head. "Okay," I tell her. "Whatever I have to do."

Although if I have to dance with Ava in gym, my chances of being voted class marshal are non-existent anyway, so either way, I won't get to lead the parade.

My mother turns to my dad. Her voice sounds sad. "We can't afford so many decorations."

My dad rubs my mom's elbow. "I think if you saw what our house would look like, you'd see the splurge was worth it."

My mother shakes her head. "It would look great. You always make our house look great. But can't you use our old decorations this year? Maybe next year, if your art career takes off, we'll be able to buy more."

"Most of the old ones are junk. They should be tossed in the garbage, not used to decorate the best house on the block."

"You can make it work." My mother points at the recycled recycling bins my father has completely stopped working on. "You'll figure out some way to recycle them." She kisses my father on the cheek, then walks out of the garage, and my dad and I are left alone.

"Guess we kind of messed up." I stand and rearrange my folding chairs.

"Big-time." My dad starts packing the Halloween supplies back into bags and boxes.

"You don't have to make the zombie maze," I tell him. "Everyone's going to Ryan's house anyway."

My dad puts his hand on my shoulder. "It ain't over till it's over." He picks up a broken old witch's broom. "Except for this." He shakes the broom. "This is over."

"Maybe you could use it for your art," I say.

My dad opens his mouth and then closes it, then opens it and closes it again. Like a fish. Or like he has some thought, but doesn't know how to say it. Finally he says, "Go get started on your letter. I've got to take this stuff back."

HUMAN DOMINOES

The next day in gym, when Mr. Lamb tells us to line up, I get in line before anyone else in my class. And when he tells us to promenade with our partners, I grab Ava's hand and get ready to go, but behind me I hear a big "Whoa!" Jamal flops forward and knocks down the boy in front of him, who knocks down the boy in front of him, who knocks down the boy in front of him, who is me.

I hear my skull crack against Ava's and a circle of pain spreads over my head, and then I topple over and my funny bone hits the floor and pain zings up my arm.

The whole thing reminds me of Human Dominoes—from my notebook. Jamal and the other two boys ask to go to the nurse's office for ice, but I tell Mr. Lamb I'm fine, even though it feels like my ankle is filled with pulsating fireballs. I hop my way through the first promenade because it hurts too much to use both feet.

Then Mr. Lamb calls out an allemande left. Ava and I grab arms and start to spin, but because I'm hopping, I go a little too fast. Then Ava has to go faster to keep up with me, and I have to hop faster to keep up with her, and before I know it we are whizzing around and my hopping foot leaves the ground and Ava is spinning me through the air.

"Whoa, whoa!" I shout. "Let me go!"

Ava lets go of my arm and I fly across the gym, land on my stomach, and spin one and a half more times on the slippery gym floor before finally coming to a stop. The banjo music Mr. Lamb plays when we dance is still floating through the speakers, and I have a great view of everyone's feet since my face is smashed against the floor. Not a single foot is moving. I tilt my head sideways and up, and see every person in my class staring at me.

Ryan Rakefield slowly claps three times. "It's a bird! It's a plane! Nope, it's Superspaz."

A few people laugh after he says it, so he keeps going. "You should make that your Halloween costume. You know, so you can be something that represents who you are. You won't even need to make up a joke for it. You'll *be* the joke."

Ava runs over and kneels down next to me. "I'm so sorry. Are you okay?"

"I'm fine." I try to stand up, but my ankle and my knee are pulsating fireballs.

Mr. Lamb sighs. "Miss Gonzales, please take your partner to the nurse's office." Ava helps me stand and has to hold my right elbow as I hop out of the gym. Behind me I hear Mr. Lamb growl, "Square-dancing is not dangerous. I don't know what's wrong with this class."

When we get to the door, Ava holds it open, and I hear Ryan Rakefield shout, "Don't forget to give your girlfriend a big thank-you kiss!"

I hop through the door, and won't let Ava hold my elbow for support when she tries to help again.

"No, thanks," I say. "I got it."

"I don't mind." She tries for my elbow again, so I hop sideways and bang my knee against a trash can. I hear a bunch of kids giggle and snicker. Behind them I see Nick with his arms tight across his chest and Thermos next to him, shaking her head.

It seems like no matter what I do, I always end up back where I started.

MISS BINKIE'S SCHOOL OF TORTURE

After school, Dad drives me to my first private dance lesson. It's a horrible end to a terrible week. We pull into the parking lot, and I groan. Miss Binkie's School of Dance has a pink-and-black-striped awning and a dancing couple painted on the front window.

"Okay," Dad says, stopping at the curb. "We'll be back in forty-five minutes. Ruby and I have a top-secret mission to perform while you are gone!"

"We do?" Ruby bounces up and down in her booster chair. "Will it be dangerous? Can we wear flashlight hats?"

I grab the edge of my seat. "You're not walking me in? How will I know what to do?"

My dad unlocks the doors. "Walk up to the front desk, tell someone your name, and they will know where you are supposed to go. Now scoot, Louie. Ruby and I don't have much time."

I open the car door as slowly as I can and inch my feet onto the pavement of the parking lot. I want to give Dad plenty of time to change his mind about forcing me to do dance lessons. This is definitely cruel and unusual punishment. No, it's worse than that: it's cruel and embarrassing punishment. I object!

I inch the door closed, but the second I hear the latch click, my dad pulls out of the parking lot and leaves me standing there in my black sweatpants. Alone.

I open the front door of the dance studio, and a thousand bells jingle above my head. Fifteen girls in leotards turn to stare at me. They stand in the lobby drinking out of matching pink water bottles. They remind me of Ari and her friends, except they don't smile.

I scrunch my shoulders and slink over to the

front desk. There is a lady there in a black leotard with a pink sweater. Her hair is scraped back into a bun on the top of her head. "Can I help you?" she asks.

I put both hands up on the counter. "What's black and pink with thirty legs and green stripes?"

The lady looks at me like I'm speaking Swahili. She smooths her hands over her bun.

"I'm Louie Burger," I say. "What's black and pink with thirty legs and green stripes?"

"Oooh." She nods knowingly as if I've somehow explained something, when all I did was say my name. She types some stuff into a computer. "I'm Miss Binkie. Your mother told me you'd be coming."

"A ballet class with runny noses." I ding the bell on the front desk since I don't have a drum to do my *ba-dum-ching*.

"What?"

"That's the answer to my joke. A ballet class with runny noses!"

"How amusing," she says, but she doesn't laugh or even smile. "Leslie is busy with another student right now." She points to a door on the left. "Please take a seat over there."

I can't believe I have to learn square-dancing from a ballerina named Leslie. I Charlie-walk over to the chair by the classroom. The door has a glass panel, so I take a quick peek before I sit down. Whoa!

There's a boy in the dance studio spinning on his head. He plants both hands on the floor and crosses his legs to the left and then the right, then he slowly lowers himself onto his belly and waves his body across the floor. When he stands up, I realize it's Jamal. Jamal from school. I didn't know he could do that. No wonder he's so good at square-dancing.

After one final spin, Jamal grabs a duffel bag and sweatshirt from the corner of the room and walks toward the door. I scramble over to the chair and hide my face behind my hands. The door opens and Jamal walks out with a huge, muscular man with a loud, booming voice. The man steps over to me and says, "You must be Louie!"

I look up and see Jamal staring at me, eyes wide, jaw dangling. I stare back, my heart thumping like the metronome ticking away in Leslie's classroom. This punishment keeps getting crueler and more embarrassing by the second. "I'm Leslie," the big man says.

Oh. Leslie is a guy, not a ballerina. He's a thousand feet tall with huge biceps. He's wearing a

striped tank top with gray sweatpants and cool gym shoes. If I wasn't in a dance studio, I'd think he was a basketball player.

"Yep, I'm Louie." I stand up and shake Leslie's hand since he's holding it out to me. And then, because it seems weird not to, I say, "Hi, Jamal."

Jamal barely looks at me. He chews his bottom lip and mumbles hello.

"You know my man Jamal? You got to help me. I keep trying to convince him to start a dance crew at—"

"Gotta go!" Jamal shouts. "My mom's here." Jamal shoves his sweatshirt inside his gym bag and takes off faster than Ari can text.

"Let's get to it!" Leslie leads me into the dance studio, and I explain to him about my coordination problem. He says it doesn't matter—even after I've banged into the piano, the wall, and the sound system.

"That's okay," Leslie says, turning off the metronome. "I like a challenge."

When the torture—I mean, lesson—is over, I

climb back into my dad's car and immediately have to cover my nose. "What's that smell?" It stinks like old shoes filled with rotten eggs and dirty diapers. Three huge black trash bags fill the way, way back of the car.

"It's for Hall—" Ruby starts to say.

"It's a surprise." Dad cuts her off. "Put it out of your head."

I pull the neck of my shirt over my nose to filter the putrid air and try to do what my dad suggests, but it's almost impossible. This stuff stinks almost as bad as my chances of getting to be class marshal. I don't know what he's planning, but I don't have a good feeling about it.

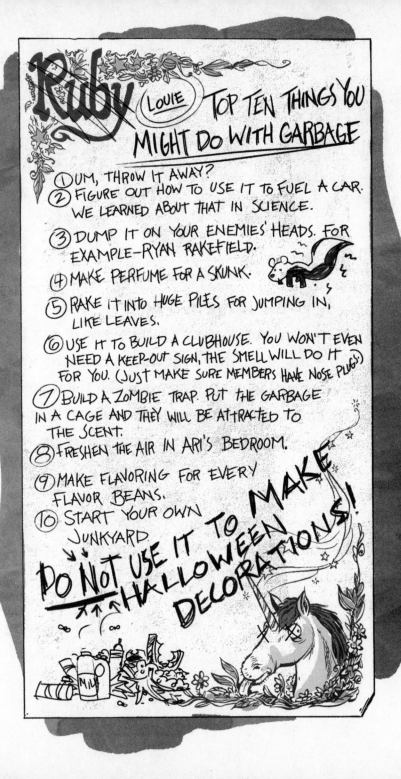

EVERYTHING IS BETTER WITH EXTRA GLITTER

Sunday is the last day I have for working on my class-marshal posters. On Monday, it will be time to hang them and then on Thursday we will have the election, and if I don't make them great today, I'm doomed. I spread my posters on half the kitchen table and Ruby spreads hers on the other side, though hers are already so covered with glitter and yarn, I don't know what more she could add. Glitter, apparently. Ruby grabs a bottle of glue and starts squeezing a squiggly pattern all around the edges of her poster. Then she shakes green glitter over the glue drizzles.

My posters are much simpler. Each has a blown-up picture from one of Charlie's movies in the center. Plus lots of smaller pictures of Charlie scattered around. I also created a border for each poster, like the kind of border Charlie used in his silent-movie title cards. But I've only done the lettering on one of the posters so far. That's what I'm working on today.

"Your posters are not very sparkly," Ruby says as she pauses mid-shake and gives my side of the table a serious once-over. She holds the tube of glitter toward me. "Here. I will share. Everything is better with extra glitter."

"No, thanks." I tilt my head and very carefully pencil in the letters *Louie: A Marshal for Modern Times!* under the picture of Charlie from his movie *Modern Times.*

Ari walks into the kitchen and grabs an apple from the fridge. She glances at the table on the way back to her room and says, "Looking good, Rubycorn."

I don't really care what Ari thinks of my posters, but she does know a lot about popularity, and I don't know anything. After the election is over, she can go back to annoying-older-sister status. Today, she may be the key to my success.

"What do you think of mine?" I call out. Ari stops in the doorway and returns to the table. "I know you said people won't know who Charlie is, but I've been working hard on educating everyone. So pretend everyone knows."

Ari studies my poster. She scrunches her mouth. She tilts her head. She takes a deep breath. She pulls out the chair next to me and sits down.

"What?!" The suspense is killing me.

Ari takes another deep breath. "Your posters are great."

"Really?" I'm surprised. I was expecting the worst. "Do you think I could win?"

She shakes her head slowly. "I didn't say that."

I scratch my head. "I'm confused."

Ruby hops off her chair and comes to stand next to me. "Your posters are good but they are the wrong way of winning." She pats my shoulder and then goes back to her seat.

I look at Ari. "Why won't I win?"

"Why do you even want to win?" Ari picks up a black marker and helps me outline the lettering I've penciled in. "You'll have way more fun marching with Nick and Thermos."

I look down at the floor. I have a feeling Ari knows about the way Ryan treats me. Ruby does, too, but I don't want to say it out loud. "I just do."

"The thing is, most kids don't want to take a risk. They don't want to be the one who votes for someone different, or makes friends with someone unusual. They go with things the way they are because that's safe. Then no one can say they are different or unusual or . . . weird."

After Ari finishes outlining all the letters, she starts coloring them in with black marker. "It's stupid and wrong, but even I do it sometimes. Like, I pretend that I think Star Wars is some geeky boy thing that I hate."

"But the Star Wars movies are your favorites." I stop coloring and stare at Ari. Why would she pretend to hate something she loves?

"They are your extra favorite," Ruby adds.

"None of my friends like them, and I don't want them to think I'm weird. It's much easier to become unpopular than popular."

Ruby shakes her head and her eyes go wide. "I hope I never get popular."

I point at her posters. "Uh, Ruby, I've got news for you. You're trying to get popular right now."

"No I'm not. I'm trying to do marching. I love marching." Ruby brushes glitter from the edge of her poster board and it lands all over the kitchen floor. Mom is not going to be happy.

Ari puts the finishing touches on the exclamation mark, then caps the marker and hands it back to me. "You might win the election and you might not," she says. "But I know that you hope winning the election will mean more than marching at the front of your class. I don't want to be mean, but that won't happen."

Ari's words settle on my chest like an elephant. "Why? Why can't it happen?"

She shrugs. "It's like I said before, kids are afraid of being different. And you won't pretend to be normal." She points at my posters, and I remember when she told me to make them about vampires or superheroes. "I'm not saying it's a bad thing. It's who you are. Sometimes I'm even jealous."

"Really?" Ari usually acts like she thinks I'm a worm.

"Yeah." Ari laughs. "*Sometimes.* Like when I see you hanging out with Nick and Thermos. You guys seem so relaxed with each other. You never have to hide your weirdness with them."

I nod. It's true. "But that won't change even if

I win the election and even if I become the most popular kid in the whole school."

Ari stands up and polishes her apple on her shirt. "You might be right. All I know is that you're in here on a Sunday afternoon, and Nick and Thermos are outside having a leaf fight on Nick's front lawn." Ari crunches her apple and walks out of the room.

I look at Ruby. She looks at her glitter. Then she tosses it on the table and runs down the hall yelling, "Mom, can I go play at Henry's house?"

A part of me wants to join her. I love a good leaf fight as much as anyone, but if I give up on trying to be class marshal, I might as well hand Ryan a tease-Louie-forever pass. I uncap my marker and start outlining the letters on my final poster.

MMMM, SHOES! DELICIOUS

On Monday, Mom drives Ruby and me to school on her way to work. We both have to go in early with our visual aids. Translation: we're in the final week of the class-marshal campaign and it's time to hang our posters. In only three days we will give our speeches and then our classes will vote, and the fate of the universe (or the fate of *my* universe) will be decided. When I get to Mrs. Adler's room, Ryan and Violet are already there. Violet has set out little note cards on each person's desk. At the top they say *Candy or Not . . . Here We Come.* Underneath she has written a list titled *Things to Do with Your Candy Besides Eat It.*

"Why would I want to do anything with my candy besides eat it?" I say, laughing. "That's like using a hundred-dollar bill as a tissue, or using a poodle as a paperweight. I mean, you could do it, but it doesn't make sense!"

"Candy rots our teeth and makes us hyperactive." Violet straightens the card on Mrs. Adler's desk. Then she tacks her poster onto the designated campaign bulletin board.

"At least *her* posters make sense." Ryan points to one of mine, featuring a picture of Charlie Chaplin's famous scene from the movie *The Gold Rush*. In it the tramp is trapped in a cabin in the woods, starving. He is so hungry he decides to eat his shoe. First he boils it, then Charlie actually eats it on camera. It's really made of licorice, but it looks totally real.

Underneath the picture of Charlie twirling his shoelaces on a fork, I've written the caption, *Vote for Me or I'll Eat My Shoe!*

"What does that even mean? Why would you eat your shoe?" Ryan rolls his eyes at me.

"It's from a movie."

"A movie that nobody's seen. Good idea." Ryan goes back to passing out mini water bottles of red fruit punch. I guess they're supposed to be blood. The labels have been peeled off and Ryan has wrapped new pieces of paper around them that say, *I'm Batty for Ryan!*

I'm so sick of Ryan always pointing out every mistake I ever make. I know I'm not perfect, but no one is. Why does he always have to pick on me? He's not making fun of Violet's posters.

"Why do you even care about my posters?" I say. Ryan looks at me, for one second his face full of surprise that I actually dared to question him. I feel surprised, too. Then he shakes it off.

"I don't care about your posters. I don't care about anything of yours." He puts another water bottle out.

"You must have cared about my notebook. Otherwise why'd you take it?"

"Yeah, well, you got it back, so what's the big deal?"

"What do you mean?"

"It's not in my desk anymore."

"Then where—" I start to say, but the first bell rings and Ryan heads to his locker to get ready for school. Did Ryan do something with my notebook? Maybe he put it back so he wouldn't get in trouble. I check my desk, but my notebook isn't there. I need to ask him where it is, but the second bell rings. The rest of our class will be inside soon.

I race to finish passing out my plastic forks with pieces of black licorice stuck on the ends. I wrote *Help Me Eat My Shoe* on the handle of every fork. At home it seemed like a great idea, but now that I'm at school, I think Ryan's right. No one's going to get it.

Everyone's going to be inside in less than a minute. I need them to know more about Charlie, to actually see the movie so that they will get my posters. I quickly grab a marker and write really big on my poster:

Come to my house tomorrow after school if you want to see Charlie eat his shoe!

I draw an arrow down to Charlie Chaplin's head as the first students start to walk into the classroom.

In a few minutes my classmates are at their desks. I watch as they notice the things Ryan, Violet, and I have put on their desks and around the room.

"Can we eat the candy?" Grant asks Mrs. Adler.

"You could donate it." Violet points to her list. "Or use it in an art project."

"Ew! I hate black licorice," Hannah says. "It's disgusting."

Mrs. Adler tells everyone that candy and drinks have to wait until lunchtime as Nick walks over to me and says, "I thought you were coming to my house tomorrow after school. To help get ready for my party."

"I am," I say.

"So why'd you invite the whole class over to your house?" He points to the invitation scrawled on my poster.

Oh. Oops. "The movie clip will be over fast. You'll come, right?"

Nick gives me a big sigh. "It's not too late, you know. You could still drop out of the race and do a three-way costume with Thermos and me."

A part of me wants to. There doesn't seem to be any chance of me ever winning. But then I'd have to accept that I'm always going to be a B.U.R.P. That Ryan is always going to make fun of me.

"I can't," I say, and his face falls.

I feel guilty, but this is something I have to do.

o o o

Tuesday after school, Nick and Thermos and I walk home with Ruby and Henry. At first no one else is with us. But when we reach the crossing guard, I hear a voice shout, "Louie, wait up!"

Ava is there with Hannah, and behind her I see Jamal walking home with . . . *Ryan Rakefield.*

Nick says, "How come she asked you to wait and not me?"

I shrug. "Maybe she knows you don't like to talk to her. Or maybe she decided to like me now. Gross, huh?"

Nick hangs his head.

"I'm sure it's just because we're going to his house," Thermos tells him. Nick shrugs.

When they catch up to us, Ryan pokes my shoulder. "I decided to make your day and watch your movie, Barfburger."

"Don't call my brother Barfburger!" Ruby puts her hands on her hips and glares up at Ryan.

He looks at her and bursts out laughing. "Nice bodyguard."

I lean down to Ruby and whisper in her ear: "Sorry, Ruby. Don't talk to him!"

I want to tell Ryan to leave, but maybe if I let him stay, he'll tell me where he put my comedy notebook. It wasn't in my locker.

When we get to my house I lead everyone to the garage. My computer is up on my stage to make the Laff Shack seem like a movie theater.

"Whoa, what's that smell?" Ryan wrinkles his nose and peers at my dad's worktable.

"Sit here," I tell them. Then I walk over to my dad. He's sorting through piles of garbage, putting anything too broken and too gross into big black garbage bags, but putting everything else in piles. He's got empty milk jugs, soda cans, and cardboard boxes. He's also got stacks of strange plastic items.

"Can you take all this stuff inside for a while, or maybe seal it up and finish washing it later?"

My dad sniffs a crusty milk carton. "I guess I've gotten used to the smell. In a few minutes you guys won't notice it anymore. Don't worry."

It's too late for worry. "Are you sure this is even going to work?" My voice is rising, but I can see Ryan fake gagging as he checks out my stage. "You've never used such smelly stuff before."

My dad picks up a tin can between two fingers and drops it in a tub of sudsy water. "I never needed so much junk at one time before. I had to get it from the recycling center. Not everyone washes their stuff before they recycle."

I glance at Ryan Rakefield, who is holding his nose. This was probably my worst idea ever. I head back over to get the movie started, but Ryan says he'll pass. "I need to get some fresh air. I thought your dad was an artist. What is he making, a garbage truck?"

"No," I scoff, like that's the most ridiculous thing I've ever heard.

"Yeah," Ruby echoes in her tough-girl voice. "He's making a zombie garbage maze!"

Ryan smirks. My heart sinks.

"*That's* what we get to do if we come to your house? I'll pass! Hey, Jamal, where do zombies score their touchdowns?" he says. "In the dead-end zone!"

He's still stealing my jokes. It makes me want to punch him in the nose. And also tape Ruby's mouth shut. And also dump a pile of garbage on my dad.

"Guess I'll be seeing everyone at my house for hot chocolate. Come on, Jamal. Let's go."

Jamal stares at me for a second. It almost looks like his eyes are apologizing, but then he says, "Yeah. Let's go. It stinks in here."

After Ryan and Jamal leave, I ask Ava and Hannah if they are ready to see the movie clip.

Ava nods her head, but Hannah says, "Actually, I forgot. I don't feel good. We have to go."

She keeps one hand over her nose as the other hand pulls Ava down the driveway.

"Henry and me are going to help clean the garbage," Ruby says. "You will like it, Henry, because sometimes we find money, but sometimes we find very special things like paper clips and bottle caps and my dad will let us keep them."

"I guess we should go get started on my birthday party," Nick says when they're gone.

"I've got to come up with some other way of introducing everyone to Charlie," I say as we walk down my driveway to Nick's house.

"But not now," Nick says. "Right? Because we are going to go to Party Warehouse to buy supplies and then we are going to set up my basement and take each other on blindfold walks."

"Right." I follow Nick and Thermos across the street but something is nagging at me. I'm sure that the solution to my problem is right in front of my nose, but I can't see it.

I try to remember everything I know about popularity and getting bumps. I think about my dad buying too much but then making everything out of garbage instead. I think about Ruby and her secret recordings for Lou Lafferman. And then it hits me.

A video!

I should make another video. Not for Lou, but for my class. I could do a mash-up of Charlie and me eating a shoe together. That would get the kids in my class to understand Charlie! And to understand me, too. But I have to do it now because the election is only two days away.

"Sorry," I say to Nick. "I'm really sorry, but I have to do something important. Go to Party Warehouse without me. I'll come over as soon as I'm done."

"What?" Nick stares at me like he doesn't quite believe he heard me right.

"Louie." Thermos says my name through clenched teeth. Her eyes bore into me like she's trying to tell me something without using words.

I know we had plans, but it's not like I'm

missing Nick's actual birthday party. I'm just missing the shopping trip for the birthday party. And when my video idea works and I'm elected marshal, I'll make it up to them.

"Sorry," I say. Then I run into my house because my idea is blazing inside my head and I don't want to lose any part of it. First I find every single fruit roll in the house, and I mold them into the shape of a shoe. Then I put my fruit shoe on a plate and take it out to the garage, where I borrow a rickety old table and chair from my dad.

"What are you doing?" Ruby asks. "Can we have a bite of your fruit-roll elephant?"

"It's not an elephant, it's a shoe," I tell her. "And you can't eat it. I need it for my video."

I race back into the house, full of energy and excitement. This is the idea that will work. This is the thing that will give me a bump. I know it. I put on my Charlie Chaplin costume, grab snacks for Ruby and Henry, and run back to the garage. As I'm Charlie-walking across my driveway I see Nick's mom pull out of his driveway with

Nick and Thermos in the backseat. I wave a big Charlie Chaplin wave, but they don't wave back.

My waddle has a little less zing when I walk back to my stage. I decide to use it. I'm supposed to be sad and starving, and not too happy about having to eat a shoe. I position our old video camera on a tripod, and set it to tape me in black-and-white because all of Charlie's movies are black-and-white. I let Ruby and Henry be my directors. When it's finished, I upload it to the computer and mix it with the clip of Charlie, so it looks like we are sharing the shoe for dinner. It takes me about three and a half hours to put the whole thing together. By the time I am done, it's dark outside and Mom is calling me to dinner. I realize that I never went over to Nick's house, but when he sees what I made, I know he'll think it was worth it.

THE BIRTHDAY BUMP

The next morning, I meet Nick on the driveway with a stack of flyers I printed out. The flyer has a picture of Chaplin, a picture of me, and the URL of my new video: *Dinner with Charlie.* I try to hand one to Nick, but he won't take it.

"I'm sorry I missed Party Warehouse," I tell him. "But watch the video. You'll see. It was worth it!"

"I'm glad you think it was worth it," he says. But he doesn't sound glad.

We start walking to school. I put his flyer back in the stack.

"Are you excited about your party?"

Nick shrugs.

"I'm very excited."

Nick looks at me out of the corners of his eyes. "Really?"

"Of course! I'm most excited for the blindfold walk. Are you still doing the thing where people grab our ankles?"

"Last night, when we were practicing, Henry stuck his hands in ice water first! I screamed."

"Awesome. I bet it felt like ghost slime."

"Yeah." Nick sort of smiles. I know he's mad at me for yesterday. I will definitely make it up to him. When I'm popular, I'll throw him a new party.

I spend the rest of the day making sure that everyone in my class has a flyer. I want them to go straight home to watch my video.

○ ○ ○

After school, I get into my costume for Nick's party. I check the computer every ten minutes to see if the number of views for my video has increased. At first, there are only a couple of views, but by the time I leave to walk over to Nick's, there are fifty-three views. Not too bad for an hour and a half.

There are only twenty-two kids in my class, so some people must have watched it more than once!

I walk across the street to Nick's house. As I head up the driveway, Grant and a bunch of other kids get dropped off. Nick and Thermos stand in Nick's doorway dressed as bacon and eggs.

"Cool video, Louie!" Grant hustles forward in his zombie-football-player costume. "Did you actually eat a shoe, or was it special effects?"

"I ate it," I tell him. "I made it out of fruit leather."

"Sooo cool." Grant holds his hand up for a high five. I've never given a high five before. I hold my hand up, too, not quite sure what to do. He slaps my palm. It stings, but I stop myself from blowing on it.

When we get inside Nick's, I can't believe it, but almost everyone tells me they saw my video. Everyone has questions for me, and three different people ask me to be their partner for the blindfold walk. I did it. I *finally* got another bump, and the timing is perfect. Thank goodness Nick's birthday falls two days before Halloween. Tomorrow is the election for class marshal. This bump could get me elected, which will give me another bump, which could give me permanent P.O.C.K.S.: Popularity Or Cool-Kid Status. The party whizzes by with kids surrounding me and wanting to be with me for every activity.

Finally, Nick blows out his candles, we eat cake and ice cream, and everyone goes home. Except for Thermos and me. The three of us sit in Nick's family room surrounded by Nick's pile of presents. I've gotten to stay and watch Nick open his presents at every single birthday of his since he was three years old. His mom gives us a pad and pencil and tells us to write everything down while she and Mr. Yamashita put Henry to bed.

"Which one do you want to open first?" I point a finger over and over again at my present. I think he's going to love it. I got him his own Three Stooges bobbleheads and a sandwich cookbook.

Nick takes off his bacon hood. "I don't feel like opening my presents."

"What?" I look around the room. Nick has three presents bigger than a microwave oven, and one that is five feet long. "Look at this haul! How can you not want to open them?"

"I don't feel like it. Okay?" Nick shoots me a dirty look. "Maybe I didn't have as good a time at my party as certain other people."

"What are you talking about?"

Thermos peels off the white gloves of her fried-egg costume and puts them on the floor. "You kind of spent the whole time talking to everyone about your new video."

"Not the whole time. I did the party activities."

"Yeah, but it's not like you were giving them your full attention." Nick scowls. "Or giving me any attention."

I blink in surprise. I don't understand why Nick is so upset. I thought he'd be happy that I was finally talking with other kids. "I'm sorry," I say, "but what was I supposed to do? Ignore everyone?"

"It's what you used to do," Nick says, "when I would ask you to hang out with us."

"No, it isn't," I remind him. "They didn't use to want me."

"You didn't use to want them. And now you don't want us." Nick points to himself and to Thermos.

How can he think I don't want them? Because I'm finally getting attention from other kids? That's crazy. "Maybe you only like me when I have no other friends besides you!"

Thermos looks shocked at my words. Nick looks disappointed.

"That's not true," he says. "I want you to have lots of friends. But are you trying to make real friends? Or are you trying to get votes?"

"It's the same thing!"

Nick shakes his head at me. "Sometimes you are really dumb."

"Dumb for liking you."

When my words are out, silence floods the space between us. Thermos looks back and forth from Nick to me like she's trying to think of something to say. Finally she tries. "Come on, you guys."

It doesn't work. If Nick doesn't even care about me spending the rest of my life getting teased, then I don't know if we can be friends anymore. "I'm going home."

I stomp home in the dark, the lights from my front porch guiding my way. I'll show Nick. I will win class marshal, and I will be the most popular boy in fifth grade and I'll make new friends and Nick will be sorry.

Instead of going inside right away, I head to my comedy stage and grab the mike.

"What's the difference between a friend and a Twinkie?" I ask my invisible audience. "A Twinkie lasts forever.

"Did you ever notice that *friend* has the word *end* in it?

"How many ex–best friends does it take to screw in a lightbulb? None. You can't trust 'em, just screw in the lightbulb yourself."

I look up at Charlie Chaplin and remember what I read in his biography. He was always lonely. He spent most of his time thinking about ways to make other people laugh and feel happy, but he was only happy when he was working.

"What do you get when you cross a friend with a railroad crossing *and* a pedestrian crossing? A double-crossing friend!"

I keep telling jokes until my anger has deflated like a used-up old balloon, then I head inside and go to bed.

VOTE FOR LOUIE, PART TWO

When I walk into school on the day of the election, a lot of kids are talking about my video. Even kids from other classes. It had four hundred views when I left for school that morning. The kids in my class must be telling people about it, and then watching it over and over again. I kind of wanted to tell Nick that on the way to school, but we didn't talk to each other. We both talked to Ruby and Henry as we walked.

After the Pledge of Allegiance, Mrs. Adler excuses Ryan, Violet, and me to go change into our costumes. When we return she lets us know that we will each have one minute to give a speech, then the class will vote, and she will announce the winner at the end of the day. Ryan goes first. As he passes by Jamal's desk on the way up to the front of the classroom, he punches Jamal in the shoulder. "Wish me luck."

Jamal rubs his shoulder. "Good luck."

I glance over at Nick. He's staring straight ahead. A part of me thinks he might know that I'm looking at him, but he won't turn around. I peer at Thermos, and she makes a sad face, then turns away.

My stomach sinks. I don't have anyone to wish me luck.

Ryan starts his speech with his back to our class, so the only thing we see is his shiny, silky black cape with its high collar. He spins around holding one arm up over his face with his eyes peeking across the top. As he slowly lowers his arm he says, "I vant to be your marshal. I vill valk vith Halloveen spirit. Vampires are the kings of Halloveen. Nothing looks as good at the head of the parade as a black cape fluttering in the breeze. I have been class marshal every year since first grade. Don't break that streak. I know how to make the parade fun with glow sticks and glow necklaces and pumpkin punching balls. Vote for me, Ryan." He raises his cape again, eyes peeking over the top, and glares around the room. "Or you vill be sorry."

"Thank you, Ryan," Mrs. Adler says as he returns to his seat. "And thank you for donating those fun supplies to our class for the parade. I want to remind everyone that any supplies donated by candidates will be part of the parade no matter who you vote for. Okay, Violet, are you ready?"

Violet nods, grabs a stack of note cards, and walks to the front of the room. She is wearing doctor scrubs and has a stethoscope hanging around her neck. "Hello, class," she says. "I'm here today because this is your chance to choose not only your class marshal but also a whole new way of looking at Halloween. Who says it has to be about getting as much candy as possible and eating it until you feel sick? This year, let's make Halloween about something good for us. Like taking a long walk with your family and friends. Instead of taking treats at every house, you could perform a trick, like double-jumping with your jump rope or walking the dog with your yo-yo. Vote for me and I'll make sure we all give away our candy and have the healthiest Halloween ever!"

Violet walks back to her seat, but only a few kids applaud as Mrs. Adler says, "Lovely ideas, Violet. Especially the part about taking a long walk with your friends and family. Okay, Louie, your turn."

I stand up, my arms and legs shaking with nerves. I used to have terrible stage fright, but now I know how to deal with it a little better. It helps me to pick one person in the room and focus on that person as I perform. The only problem is Nick won't look at me. He's staring out the window and Thermos keeps giving me sad eyes.

I waddle up to the front of the room like Charlie Chaplin. My stomach does flip-flops. I guess my stage-fright cure only works if there is someone in the audience I trust. I feel certain that pretty soon everyone in the room will be my friend. But that doesn't really help me right now.

I put a hand on my stomach to settle it and

push a button on the class computer. Old-fashioned piano music fills the room, like the kind in Chaplin's silent movies. I am going to do a silent speech.

Jamal's expression changes when the music starts playing. He goes from bored to curious, and maybe a little worried. I don't trust him and he doesn't make my stomach feel any better, but for some reason I decide to look at him as I give my speech.

I waddle to the middle of the room, twirling my cane and adding in a few funny hop steps. When I am facing my class, I hold up the first poster:

I would like to be your class marshal.

I put the poster down and Charlie-march around the room as if I am leading a parade.

Like the tramp, I may sometimes seem small and unimportant...

I shrink my head down between my shoulders and look around the room as if I'm kind of embarrassed.

But, like the tramp, I take all my jobs very seriously!

I pretend to clean the classroom, sweeping, organizing, dusting. I even dust Mrs. Adler.

I already ate my shoe, but if you vote for me...

I kneel, clasp my hands, and pretend I'm pleading with everyone.

I'll march until I wear out my legs.

Then I do a trick that isn't a Charlie Chaplin move, but it fits the moment. I march back and forth in front of the room bending my knees as I go, so it looks like I'm getting smaller and smaller. At the moment the music ends, I plop onto the floor, then I pop back up and take a bow.

Mrs. Adler says, "Very interesting, Louie. I don't think I've ever seen anyone give a speech without talking before."

The class claps and I walk back to my seat. Mrs. Adler passes out the ballots, and I write my name on the slip of paper, waddle up to the box on Mrs. Adler's desk, and drop my vote in. As I return to my desk, I notice a lot of people staring at me, but I don't know if they are staring in a good way or a bad way. I don't know how I am going to wait the entire day to find out what happened.

AND THE WINNER IS...

The day drags by. At lunch, I sit with Grant and his friends. Grant tells me he voted for me, but no one else does. He and his friends try to include me in their conversation, but they mostly want to talk about tryouts for travel basketball. When I ask them who would win in a breakfast-food wrestling match, a Belgian waffle or a hard-boiled egg, they laugh, but they don't try to figure it out the way Nick and Thermos would. I imagine their answers: "Well, the egg would roll away any time the waffle got close, so he can't be beat," Nick would say. "Yeah," Thermos would answer, "but if the waffle does one body slam, *boom*, egg salad."

I sigh and look at their end of the table. Thermos says something and makes a silly face. Nick laughs until he sees me looking, then he presses his lips together and turns his head away. Behind me, I hear Ryan talking loudly at the other table.

"Doesn't he even know that a speech is supposed to involve speaking? That was the dumbest thing I've ever seen."

I freeze. Ryan's words make me want to shrink down again like I did in my speech. I hope I win. I hope that quiets him for good.

"Yeah." I hear a bunch of voices behind me agree. The guys at my table keep talking basketball. Maybe they don't hear what Ryan is saying, or maybe they pretend they don't.

"I don't know," one person says to Ryan. "There was something sort of okay about it."

"You think silent dorks are cooler than vampires?"

"Forget it," the voice says. "His speech was kind of cool, that's all. I liked the funny walk." I can't believe it. One of Ryan's friends is actually complimenting me.

"Probably because you think it's like square-dancing, *pardner*. You should change your Halloween costume to a cowboy. Or maybe you should be a ballet dancer since we know you used to take lessons."

I sneak a look over my shoulder at Ryan's table and see Jamal sitting next to Ryan with his cheek resting in the palm of his hand. I didn't know he stopped taking dance lessons. He was so good.

"Never mind," Jamal says. "It doesn't matter. I'm sure you're going to win anyway."

"Of course I'm going to win. You guys voted for me, right?"

Everyone at his table says yes.

As I look away I wonder what it would feel like to have a whole table of friends like that. Who you *knew* would vote for you, no matter what. I have no idea who Nick and Thermos voted for. The lunch bell rings and I gather my stuff up and head back to class.

o o o

With ten minutes to go before the end of the day, Mrs. Adler picks up the ballot box from her desk. My hands fill with tingles. This is it. My life is either going to change or I'll have to accept that I was meant to be a B.U.R.P. forever and ever.

"It was a close race," Mrs. Adler tells us. "The candidates were separated by only four votes."

Yeah, yeah, yeah. Teachers always say that stuff, like everyone's a winner or something. But closeness doesn't matter. Even if you lost by only one vote, you still lost. The only kid that matters is the one who gets to march at the front of the line.

"This year's class marshal is—" Mrs. Adler looks around the room smiling. Her eyes stop at me and my breath catches in my throat. I cross my fingers. "Louie Burger!"

"Yes!" My fist shoots up into the air. I want to dance around the room, but I know that wouldn't be good sportsmanship, so I let my feet wiggle under my desk. A bunch of kids say, "Congratulations, Louie!" and "Good job." My whole body feels fizzy like a shaken-up bottle of ginger ale, and I want to blow my lid off and celebrate. The thing is, I can't tell if anyone in the room is excited enough to cheer with me.

The kids in my classroom have different expressions. Some smile at me, like Grant and Mason. Some won't look at me, like Thermos and Nick. Some are scowling, like Ryan, but Jamal has a strange expression, like he just heard a joke and can't decide if it's funny. Mrs. Adler nods at me proudly. Unfortunately, no one, not a single person, looks super happy for me. It kind of pops some of my fizz bubbles.

When the bell rings, Thermos says halfheartedly, "I'm glad you get to be marshal, Louie. You'll do a great job."

"Thanks," I say, wanting the conversation to continue, but she walks away to catch the bus. I head outside to meet Nick, Henry, and Ruby.

"Ruby gets to be our class march-al," Henry announces. "That means she marches first."

"It's *marshal*, Henry," Nick says. Then he holds his hand up to Ruby for a high five. She jumps up and slaps it. "Awesome job, Ruby," Nick says. "I'm so happy for you!"

I try not to think about the fact that Nick is happier for my sister than he is for me.

"Ruby's going to be the best march-al in the world. And I will march right behind her and say, 'March, Ruby, march! March, Ruby, march!'"

"Thank you, Henry. You can be my assistant

march-al, and next year I will tell everyone that you should be march-al and I will be your assistant."

Ruby paws her feet at the ground and marches at the same time. It's strange, but I guess that's the look she's going for. "March, Henry, march. March, Banoonicorn, march!"

Henry starts doing the prancing-unicorn thing, too, and the two of them march off ahead of us, leaving me and Nick walking alone.

"Guess you got your wish," he says. "Congratulations."

"Thanks," I tell him. "I just wish you understood why I wanted to win."

Nick shuffles through a big pile of leaves on the sidewalk. "I do understand. But I don't think it's as important as you do."

I don't know what to say. I don't think he's right, but I don't know how to defend myself. We say goodbye and go home. Tomorrow is going to be a very strange Halloween.

o o o

I'm sitting in the middle of my stage polishing my Chaplin shoes and wondering if Charlie Chaplin felt this lonely when he was on top of the world, when my dad puts his paintbrushes in the utility sink and says, "Trade those tramp shoes in for dancing shoes, buddy. It's time for your last lesson."

I stand up and notice, for the first time, that Dad has completely transformed the garbage. I don't know what he's transformed it into, but I see plenty of strange sculptures made out of milk

cartons and garbage bags. They're creepy, that's for sure, and they don't smell anymore, so that's a plus. But I have no idea what they are.

Dad catches me looking and says, "They're not done yet."

"What are they?" I ask.

"You'll see. They're a surprise. It will be done by the time your class gets here."

Right. My class. I forgot they are coming over to my house after the parade. That lifts my spirits a little. Even if winning didn't feel the way I thought it would, I'm sure that after the parade and the party it will feel different. Probably then I'll feel like the king of the world.

Dad and Ruby drive me to my last dance lesson. When I get there, Jamal is finishing up his session. I'm surprised to see him. I thought Ryan said Jamal was done with dance. I wait in the chair next to the door and when Jamal comes out he mumbles hello and scurries past me, but I call out his name. He turns and looks at me.

"What are you doing here?" I ask, jogging over to him.

He looks at me like I asked him what color the sky is. "Break-dance lessons. Duh."

"Didn't I hear Ryan say you stopped taking lessons? Did you start again?"

Jamal's eyes dart around the room. "Do not tell anyone you saw me taking lessons." He leans his head in close. "I mean it!"

"But you're great. I've seen you through the window."

"Ryan cannot know. You have to swear you won't tell. He will tease me for the rest of my life." Jamal grabs on to my arm and stares into my eyes. He means business, I can tell.

"I thought you guys were friends. Can't you ask him not to talk about dancing? Tell him it bugs you."

Jamal pulls his head back and makes a face. "You don't know anything about friendship," he says, "if you think that would work."

"I guess not," I say as Jamal hoists his gym bag over his shoulder and walks out of the dance studio. I think about what Jamal said. I know I don't know a lot about friendship—I haven't had too many friends over the years—but I know Nick and Thermos and I would never say mean things to each other on purpose, even if we sometimes do by accident. And we don't make each other hide stuff we like doing. That sounds like Ari's friends.

Without even thinking about it, I waddle into Leslie's room like Charlie Chaplin.

"Hey," Leslie says. "What's that?"

"Oh." I stop, embarrassed. He must think I was trying to dance and doing it wrong again.

"Was that a Charlie Chaplin impression?"

I nod. I can't believe Leslie knows about Charlie. "I love imitating old comedians," I tell him. "I can do a little Buster Keaton, Charlie, Harpo, and my friends and I can do a Three Stooges–style slap fest no problem."

"You know, those great old physical comedians

were quite graceful. If you can imitate them, then you should have no problem figuring out how to dance."

Leslie shows me the steps again, but this time he does them as if Charlie Chaplin were dancing. Then he has *me* do the steps as Charlie. When I do it that way, somehow it's easy for me to move my feet without tripping or falling.

"Great!" Leslie gives me a fist pump. Then he turns on the country music and we square-dance around the room.

When it's almost time to leave, Leslie turns off the music and I grab my coat. "So who are these awesome friends you have who know how to do a Three Stooges slap fest? They sound like they really get you."

I nod and imagine what it would have been like to trick-or-treat as Curly, Larry, and Moe. Ringing doorbells, then poking each other in the eye. Picking out candy, then whacking each other with our candy-filled pillowcases. I try to picture myself trick-or-treating as Charlie and all I can see is the tramp's back as he waddles down the street, alone.

I say goodbye to Leslie and head out to the front of the studio, where my dad is waiting for me. I get in the car, and as Dad drives home I come up with a plan.

TOAST FOR HALLOWEEN

When I get home from dance, I go straight to Louie's Laff Shack, of course. It's still the best place to do my thinking. It's a little creepy now because it's filled with my dad's Halloween decorations. I try to ignore the vampires, witches, and mummies staring at me from his side of the room. Here's what I think: a video got me into this, so maybe a video can get me out.

This time I do one of my favorite Three Stooges shorts. One that's perfect for Halloween. It's called *We Want Our Mummy*. In it, the Three Stooges are wandering through an ancient tomb looking for a mummy, when they get separated. Curly wanders around the tomb calling out for Moe and Larry,

but he keeps running into spooky things like skeletons and mummies. That's the part I act out. Thankfully, my dad's Halloween decorations are all over the garage, so it's easy to make my stage look like a haunted tomb.

I pretend to run around the tomb looking for Moe and Larry, like Curly did in the film. "Hey, Moe! Hey, Larry, where are you?"

Then, like Curly, I realize there is an echo. "Where are you?"

Where are you?

"I asked you first!"

I asked you first!

"I wish we were still the Three Stooges."

You shouldn't have switched your costume.

Just like Curly I act surprised and scared when the echo answers instead of repeating.

Then I add a few touches of my own that weren't in the original short. I bump into skeletons, mummies, and spooky trees. Each time, I say Curly's *woob-woob-woob* catchphrase and look around like

I want to poke someone in the eye or slap them on the nose, but no one is there. Finally, I look into the camera and say, in my best Curly voice, "It soytenly is no fun being Curly without Moe and Larry." I bark a Curly bark and turn off the camera.

While my video is uploading to the Internet, I e-mail Mrs. Adler and tell her that I no longer want to be Halloween marshal. I ask her if it's okay for the runner-up to walk in my place. I'd rather walk with Nick and Thermos if they'll still have me.

After my video is posted online, I message Nick and Thermos and ask them to please watch it.

Finally, I pack up my Charlie Chaplin costume and the paper mustaches I made to pass out at the parade. I ask my dad if he'll help me with a new costume. It's part of my surprise for Nick and Thermos.

When Ruby sees me getting rid of my costume, she asks me if she can have it.

"Aren't you being a unicorn?" I ask. "Oh right. I mean a loony-corn."

"Uh-huh," she says. "I need it for my loonicorn costume."

I give it to her. It would take too long to figure out what she could possibly be talking about.

○ ○ ○

When I wake up the next morning, the first thing I do is check our computer. There are two new messages for me. One from Nick that says, *Cool video*, and one from Thermos that says, *The Three Stooges are the best!*

At school, we still have to learn and do work, even though it's Halloween. There should be a law against that. It's impossible to concentrate on normal things like writers' workshop and social studies when you know there is going to be a parade and a party and trick-or-treating in the afternoon. But Mrs. Adler says we have to concentrate, there's still a lot of school to get through before Halloween. Including gym. Mr. Lamb rearranged our schedule because of the parade.

As my class gets in line for gym, Mrs. Adler

calls me to her desk. "I got your e-mail, Louie. Are you sure?"

I nod. "I'll enjoy the parade a lot more if I march with my friends."

Mrs. Adler looks thoughtful, then says, "Okay, if you're sure. I'll tell Ryan."

My heart falls a little bit as I get in line. I was sort of hoping Violet was runner-up. Oh well. I guess the expression that fits here is: *Can't win 'em all.*

When we get to gym, Mr. Lamb tells us that today is our square-dance hoedown party. He calls it a party, but I know it's a test. He's going to be watching us to make sure we learned all the square-dance moves. I guess it doesn't even matter anymore, since I'm not going to be marshal, but I'm kind of proud that I can do the dance steps. I want to do a good job on the assessment. I want my mom to be proud.

We get in our squares and Mr. Lamb starts the music. When it's time to promenade around the room, I promenade like Charlie Chaplin. When it's time to do-si-do, I imagine I'm Curly in one of the Three Stooges' crazy Russian-dancing scenes. And when I weave the ring, I imagine I'm Buster Keaton being blown around the circle in a big storm.

"Mr. Burger!" Mr. Lamb growls when my group is through. I flinch, thinking he's going to yell at me, but he actually smiles. "Most improved. And I like the way you've added your own flourishes."

I pretend to tip my hat to Mr. Lamb.

"Wow, Louie. You didn't step on my foot even once," Ava says.

"Thanks!" I say. "I pretended your feet were deadly poison. It was easy to imagine."

"Oh." Ava looks confused. "Good idea."

"Looks like Mr. Lamb found a new cowboy." Ryan sidles up behind me and whispers his words at the back of my neck. It almost makes me sorry about my decision not to be marshal. "Too bad your dancing is funnier than your jokes."

I turn around and look at Ryan and for the first time I see what he truly is. He's not the most popular boy in fifth grade. As a matter of fact, I don't think he has any real friends.

"You're a joke, Louie, and you know it. I bet that's why you chickened out of being marshal."

Ryan taunts me, bawking like a chicken. A couple of the kids he bosses around are laughing and bawking, too, but as I watch them, I realize they're not even looking at me. They're looking at Ryan. They aren't making fun of me, they are copying Ryan and hoping he won't make fun of them. Suddenly, I don't feel like a B.U.R.P. anymore. I feel like S.W.A.B.: Someone With A Backbone.

I look at Ryan and nod. "I guess you're right," I say, and then I start bawking and strutting like a chicken. Ryan keeps bawking at me, but I bawk back until I can tell he's lost—he doesn't know what to do anymore. Finally, he says, "Whatever," and walks away.

o o o

At lunch, anyone whose parents sent in a permission slip is allowed to go home to change into their costume. Nick and I walk home with Ruby and Henry.

"I can't believe you aren't going to be marshal." Nick shakes his head. "I voted for you, you know."

"You did?"

"Sure. Even when I'm mad at you, you're still my best friend."

"Well, thanks," I say. "But you were right, marching with you and Thermos will be way better."

"Too bad about the Three Stooges, though," Nick says. "Maybe next year."

I hide my smile. It's true we can't do our Three Stooges costume, but Nick doesn't know I've got a great surprise planned.

We say goodbye when we get to our houses, and I race inside. I eat a quick Fluffernutter for lunch and then I put on my new costume. Toast! I'm a piece of perfectly browned delicious buttered toast. Dad helped me make it out of a leftover cardboard box. It'll go perfectly with Nick and

Thermos's bacon-and-eggs costume. I can't wait to see the looks on their faces. I tell Dad I'm ready to go back to school, but he's in my sister's room helping Ruby with her unicorn costume. Her shoe is stuck in one of her hooves.

"Why don't you go on ahead, Louie?" my dad suggests. "I'll walk Ruby back to school. I want to see the parade anyway."

When I get to school, the classes are lining up with their teachers outside on the blacktop. There is a set of risers for the grand marshal competition and when that's finished, we will march around the school and down six neighborhood streets before returning for the sing-along. Then it's home for trick-or-treating!

I scan the kids gathering in the fifth-grade area.

I see Ryan in his vampire costume, Violet in her doctor suit, and Ava and Hannah's two peas in a pod. I see a zombie football player, a sumo wrestler, a whoopee cushion, and fancy witches, but I don't see bacon and eggs anywhere. Maybe they aren't here yet. I turn around to look at the students who are still arriving, and I see two Charlie Chaplins walking right toward me. They are doing the Charlie-walk perfectly and even though I wanted people to learn it, I feel a little angry that someone stole my costume idea. I mean, I know I changed my costume to toast, but whoever it is didn't know that I was going to switch. I stomp over to them to give them a piece of my mind.

It's Nick and Thermos. Whoa!

"What happened to bacon and eggs?" I say.

"We wanted to match with you," Nick says.

"What happened to Charlie?" Thermos asks.

I guess they had the same surprise idea that I did. "Two Charlie Chaplins and a piece of toast is the worst group costume in the history of costumes." I shake my head at us.

"I don't know," says Nick, grinning. "I kind of like it. It reminds me of a sandwich."

"Everything reminds you of a sandwich." Thermos twirls her cane.

"It works," I say. "We're a reverse comedian

sandwich. Bread in the middle, comedians on the outside." It might not be the best costume, but I'm sure it's the most unique.

Principal Newton turns on the sound system and asks everyone to line up so we can choose our grand marshal. I look at the risers and groan. Ruby's costume is . . . I don't even know what she could possibly be. Nick, Thermos, and I might be only the second most unique.

Ruby is wearing a curly orange clown wig and my giant Charlie Chaplin shoes. She's got the Charlie bowler hat on, but it has a unicorn horn sticking out the top of it. A long white sparkly tail hangs from beneath the Charlie jacket, and she's sort of wearing a Charlie mustache, except hers is white and sparkly instead of black. The principal goes down the line of marshals, holding the microphone up to each person and asking them to describe their costume. After each person says what their costume is, their class cheers. When he gets to Ruby, she announces, "I'm Cornelia Louie Charlie Chaplin Rubycornica! Because unicorns are awesome and my brother is my most popular Charlie in the world."

Ruby's class cheers for her, but Nick, Thermos, and I cheer louder.

Principal Newton puts on a rainbow stovepipe hat, which he says is his choosing cap. He closes his eyes and hops up and down on one foot. Then he says, "I can't explain it. It's certainly the strangest costume I've ever seen, but for pure originality, this year, the grand marshal will be Ruby Burger!"

I hoot and cheer for Ruby as loud as I can. When she waddles to the front of the line and Charlie-skids around the corner of the school, the Charlie-walk leading the parade looks every bit as good as I imagined it would.

After school, Thermos comes home with Nick and Henry and Ruby and me, and I almost faint when I get to my house. My dad has set up gnarled trees all over our driveway, with spooky cotton spiderweb walls making a maze for people to walk through. There is a sign at the beginning:

TRICKS THIS WAY $\rightarrow$

$\leftarrow$ **TREATS THAT WAY**

"Whoa!" I say. My dad breathes on his fingernails, then buffs them against his shoulder. "Not too shabby, huh, Louie?"

Nick, Thermos, and I try the maze, while Ruby
and Henry go for the treats. At the first turn, a
mummy with moving eyes seems to watch us as
we pass, and I scream. But so do Nick and Thermos. It's a fun kind of terrifying. At each turn
something else pops out or falls down on us:

278

spiders, ghosts, bats, and, at the very end, a giant unicorn with smoke coming out of its nostrils that snorts at us.

"Barftacular!" I tell my dad.

"Super spectacular," says my mom, who's dressed as Super Mom. "And you did it under budget, too. That's even more amazing." She gives my dad a huge hug.

"OMG!" Ari and her friends, dressed as sparkly pink witches, run out of the house clutching their cell phones. "Louie's video has, like, over five thousand hits."

"I thought it had more than that already," Mom says.

"No, I mean his new video." Ari holds up her phone.

"New video?" Dad looks at me with his eyebrows raised.

I back away slowly. Was I supposed to get permission? Oops. "Who's that?" I say, pointing. "Mr. Armbruster?"

We look at the end of the driveway. It's not

Mr. Armbruster. It's Jamal and Ava. They don't actually seem to be walking together, just next to each other.

"Hi," I say. "I thought everyone was going to Ryan's house now that he's the marshal."

"Most people are." Jamal shrugs. "I saw your video online. Your mummy stuff looked pretty cool. I wanted to see it for real."

"Thanks. My dad made it."

"You changed your costumes." Ava points at Nick, Thermos, and me. "Your new one reminds me of a sandwich."

"That's what I said!" Nick shouts. Then he realizes he talked to Ava. Like a regular person. He stares at the driveway. *"Olive snarbwichkes,"* he mumbles.

"What?" Ava asks.

Nick clears his throat. "I love sandwiches."

Ava beams. "Me, too!"

Jamal leans over to me and whispers, "I wanted to give this back to you. Ryan took it, not me. But

I stole it from him. I didn't read the whole thing. Just the parts he made me listen to."

Jamal hands me a plastic trick-or-treat bag with my comedy notebook in it.

"Thanks," I say.

"Thanks for keeping my secret," he says.

"Are you going to Ryan's now?" I ask Jamal.

He shrugs again. "I guess. I don't have anyone else to trick-or-treat with."

"You could trick-or-treat with us," I tell him.

"Really? You'd let me come with you?"

"Sure." I look over at Thermos chasing Ruby and Henry around the lawn. "And maybe someday you could shoot baskets with Thermos. She's good."

"Way better than me!" He laughs. "No problem."

"OMG!" Ari and her friends shout. They run toward the street.

I turn around and see the Channel Seven News van pulling up in front of my house. A reporter and a cameraman step out. The reporter asks,

"Is this the house with the decorations made out of garbage?"

"Yes!" my mother says, putting down the candy bowl filled with raisins and pretzels. "This is the artist right here." She grabs my dad and pulls him over to the reporter.

My dad looks stunned. "How did you know about me?"

"Someone forwarded me your video," the reporter says.

"My video?" He looks at me and I shrug.

She pulls out her phone, presses a few buttons, and I hear my tinny voice squeaking, "Moe! Larry! Where are you?"

Then the cameraman points at me and says, "Hey, aren't you the boy doing the Curly impression?"

"No!" I back away from the camera. I've had enough of fame and fortune. I look at Nick and Ava, Thermos and Jamal, Ruby and Henry, and even Ari and her coven of witchy friends. That's plenty enough people for me. "Can't talk now! I'm going trick-or-treating."

We step out into the street filled with other trick-or-treaters. The air smells like bonfires and hot chocolate and best friends. I love Halloween.